Lip Smackin' Good

Lip Smackin' Good

Natalie Weber

www.urbanbooks.net

Urban Books, LLC
97 N18th Street
Wyandanch, NY 11798

ISBN 13: 978-1-60162-590-8
ISBN 10: 1-60162-590-1

First Trade Paperback Printing April 2014
Printed in the United States of America

10 9 8 7 6 5 4 3 2 1

This is a work of fiction. Any references or similarities to actual events, real people, living or dead, or to real locales are intended to give the novel a sense of reality. Any similarity in other names, characters, places, and incidents is entirely coincidental.

Distributed by Kensington Publishing Corp.
Submit Wholesale Orders to:
Kensington Publishing Corp.
C/O Penguin Group (USA) Inc.
Attention: Order Processing
405 Murray Hill Parkway
East Rutherford, NJ 07073-2316
Phone: 1-800-526-0275
Fax: 1-800-227-9604

Lip Smackin' Good

Natalie Weber

Acknowledgments

First, I would like to thank all my fans for supporting me. There would be no me if there was no you.

Thanks to my editors, you are definitely a dream to work with.

Thanks to my dearest husband for putting up with my abandonment at times. I couldn't continue to do this if you weren't in my corner. Love you unconditionally.

Lastly, thanks to Urban Books for all your hard work. Lonnie, Karen and Jeff especially. Love you like cooked food.

Natalie

Cindy

1

"A'ight, bitch, this is how yo' first night gonna work..."

This bitch can't be serious. I looked at her cockeyed. "Umm, excusa'me?" I sure as hell didn't want to start any shit 'cause heaven knew I needed this to work out. Working that bullshit home aide crap wasn't cutting it for me. So I made sure my attitude was still sweet when I asked.

"So, ain't nobody school you?" the fire-red-haired, Amazon-looking chick asked.

There I stood with a hot pink string up my ass, neon green net dress over it, my 38-Cs perky as ever, and glitter on damn near every inch of my body. I didn't have my heels on yet, just some sandals, but shit if she wanted to throw down then so be it. When Sherry told me about this place she definitely didn't tell me nothing about this fuckin' bitch. I knew this was a ghetto spot, but I had to see how this shit really was before I went out of state. *Now here we go with this chick. This bitch killing my vibe.*

"Well, this is how it works. All the money you make tonight I get a small percentage," Big Red said, smiling ear to ear.

Oh, really! No, this chick didn't just say she gets a percentage of my fucking money. From the looks of it she must be the queen bee in here. The only reason she was tryin'a take my money was because her ass older than my mother and couldn't make none of her own. Biting my bottom lip so I wouldn't start laughing in her face, I played like a foreigner. "*Qué?*"

She slowly reached for my bouncy curl hanging down the side of my face; her voice determined how serious she was. "You heard what I said. Bitch, I know where you from. You probably could've gotten over on the next chick, but you sure as hell gonna respect my ass. I don't give a shit. There's rules in this game, newbie."

Stepping back a bit, I looked around to see if there was anything I could pick up to hit this bitch with just in case she wanted to brawl. Like a kid caught stealing from the cookie jar my eyes darted about and I asked the obvious: "So what if I don't make any money then what?"

"Oh, trust me you gonna make some money tonight. Let all these niggas in here see they got some new pussy to smell. They gonna be hitting that ATM out back just to get a whiff of what you got." Her eyes stared at my nipples peeking through the holes in my dress.

"I see." I turned around, putting my back to her 'cause I wasn't about to get hit in the face. I never fought anyone naked, but I sure wasn't gonna let this big bitch get over on me. *I'ma kill Sherry when I see her ass.* I saw the glass candle holder on the small counter space in front of me. Some of my makeup was on the counter, too, and I started fiddling with the compact mirror. I opened it, positioning it perfectly to see if she would swing. Damn, if this chick hit me I had to be fast, duck and clock her ass over her head with the candle holder.

Before Big Red could even say another word, a short, older white, eight-month-pregnant-looking man with sunglasses on strolled in with a wide grin. Quickly I turned around to see Big Red in a hurry to greet him. *Damn, he could be her father.* I didn't have a clue as to who he was. His gray hair had a Donald Trump comb over and he looked like he belonged on some casino floor in Vegas. All the ladies flocked to him. I was the only one just watching the scene. He moved around the room groping every girl he passed: pats on their asses, kisses on their cheeks, even rubbing his fat, little, nubby hands across their breasts to help perk their nipples up. I could see him getting closer. I purposely turned my back toward him and just started fidgeting with everything on the countertop in front of me.

"And you must be Cindy." His arms opened wide ready to feel my goods.

Oh, no, we ain't playing that game. Reaching down toward my travel suitcase hoping to avoid those touchy-feely hands of his, I answered, "Yes." I made sure to put my best smile on. I prayed that it was good enough.

"Well, aren't you a doll. Stand up and let me take a good look at you." He put his hand out to help me to my feet.

His hand felt clammy. I couldn't run, I couldn't hide, so I complied and took his hand. When I got to my feet I quickly stepped to the side and shook my tits from side to side. As I displayed my goods I could see Frank approaching. He was the guy who hired me.

"Cindy, what's your stage name going to be?"

Taking the opportunity to remove myself from the room I said, "Am I up first?"

"Frank, aren't you going to introduce us?" the older bald man asked.

"Lou, we don't have the time for this. You can see her when she's up there. Didn't Sam talk to you about that shit?" Frank asked annoyed.

Hearing the slight tension in his voice I tried to step away.

"Cindy, what's your stage name going to be?" Frank asked again.

Now it seemed that he was annoyed at me. "Let's see, how about Candy?"

"Are you asking me or answering me? Cindy, I really don't care what the fuck you call yourself. Shit, as long as you keep this place packed for at least the next few weeks you can call yourself whatever you like. Lou, come on; let these girls get to work." Tugging on Lou to leave, Frank nudged him out after a couple of minutes.

I sat there waiting for Big Red to approach me again after Frank and Lou left, but she didn't. Watching all those ladies letting that old man fondle them in every which way was disgusting. I cringed at the thought. I wanted to barf, literally. But, it was hypocritical of me to feel that way when I was there to allow who knew who to do the very same to me. I shook my head.

There had to be another way to make this work. I wasn't about to sell drugs and selling my pussy could kick rocks. Sex was the biggest hustle and the compensational benefits was a must. From all I'd heard it was certainly easy money for years if you did it correctly. Shit, I couldn't depend on that sorry-ass nigga Wayne. I glanced down at my watch; it was almost ten. *If this nigga ain't here by ten his ass gots to go.* Trying to convince myself that it would be the last chance he had with me. I kept repeating the words in my head: *His ass gots to go . . . His ass gots to go . . .*

I loved Wayne to death; he was my first and only love I had known. But lately it had been the same shit just different days. His little stickups weren't getting us shit. It was survival only; none of it produced enough money to really evolve. It just held us together for the moment or six months tops.

My head was spinning and my stomach was tied in knots. This was my first time ever doing this in front of total strangers. I had danced a million times for Wayne, even put that shit on video. But it wasn't the dancing I was scared of; it was the hands and the slaps on the ass that I was nervous about. Asking Wayne to be out there would make it a whole easier.

I paced a bit before I looked into the crowd from the side stage. I couldn't see anyone completely; everything was a bit dark. I blinked my eyes a few times to adjust then I saw him sitting at the bar talking to one of the dancers. From his smiles and head tilts I knew she was throwing him everything he wanted to hear: compliments fit for royalty.

Wayne had soft, curly black hair, light eyes, and chocolate-toned skin. His height was average, but his well-formed abs and defined muscles made up for that. When I first met him he was eighteen and I was almost sixteen; my sixteenth birthday was only days away. He was skinny and his hair wasn't even cut on a regular basis. The people we knew back then wouldn't even recognize him now.

I stared at him sitting there looking as fine as ever. I couldn't be mad at the chick chatting him up. *If I see anything more from his ass I swear there's gonna be more than a striptease happening.* Sherry, my best friend, was sitting at one of the tables close to the stage. That's my girl; she's always there to support a chick.

My stomach was still in knots. *Why in the world did I even say I would do this shit?* Suddenly I felt a slight slap on my ass. "What—"

"It's time, Candy. The DJ will be announcing your name in a few. You ready to make some money?" Frank hollered.

Before I could even answer his ass, I heard the music lowered and the announcement that new pussy was in the house. Well not in those terms, but he might as well have said it straight up. Since the music was lowered I could hear the shuffling of feet and movement to get a look at the stage before them.

I took a deep breath and walked out onto the stage ready to shake my ass. I just had to make sure not to stay in one spot to long. *Lawd knows they gonna have their hands ready to feel everything.*

Sherry

2

Shit! Shit! Shit! This bitch gonna make these niggas go insane. I could only smile as I tossed twenty singles in the air and watched them land all over Cindy's half-naked body. If only she had listened to me a long time ago, her ass would be making even more money now and damn sure wouldn't be in this shithole. I had to admit seeing her like that—opening her legs wide, exposing her bald kitty, grinding on that pole, and shaking her fat ass—got me more than a little excited.

Yeah, sure I'd been with girls before, but no one ever made me feel like this. My pussy started to throb. I had to sit back down before I reached out and touched her like most of these men. Trying not to stare as she did her thing, I grabbed a hold of my drink to keep my hands occupied. All the girls I'd been with were just threesomes with my boyfriends. It was never anything serious like a one-on-one type thing. She's been my girl for years. I've been around her for years. Where did all this come from?

Trying to keep my eyes off Cindy, I turned my head toward the bar. I could see Wayne's stupid ass smiling and profiling next to some big-tittie bitch, acting like he really bought a drink. Please, I knew for a fact that Cindy made sure to give him money to tip her. *Let me go break this shit up before she jump off that stage and start some drama.* I couldn't for the life of me figure out why she kept getting back with this dude. He sucked ass!

"Hey, Wayne . . ." The "oh shit I'm caught" look flushed his face when I tapped his shoulder. I snuck up on his ass.

"Oh, shit, Sherry? I ain't think you was gonna be here otherwise I would've came with you."

"Whatever, Wayne, you full of shit. Why you ain't over there throwing them dollars in your pockets for your girl up there?" I sucked my teeth and rolled my eyes. He was pathetic.

"Oh shit, I didn't even realize that she was on." He turned around and stared at the stage.

"Well, maybe if you wasn't trying so hard to be the player you woulda heard the announcement, jackass!" I was so pissed at him. I should have slapped him for Cindy.

"I wasn't doing nothing; this bitch just rolled up on me looking for a sucker," he said, quickly jumping off the stool and shifting away from the 36-Ds he was so nestled up to a minute ago.

I laughed when the chick stuck her middle finger up at him and walked away. I rolled my eyes at him and walked toward the bathroom. He was such an idiot. I knew I shouldn't have drunk that bottle of water. I just hoped there was a lock on the bathroom stall. I got the bartender's attention and asked, "Excuse me, where's the ladies' room?"

"There's only one next to the VIP room, toward the back."

Now what kind of place is this? How this place only gonna have one fuckin' bathroom? "You can't be serious. Thanks." Now that's just stupid. I hurried my little ass past all the horny men because I was almost pissing on myself. It was so dark in the back. I could still hear the music from the main floor, but not loud enough to drown out the moans and groans coming from the VIP room. I saw a glowing sign for the restroom right next to it. I really had to go to the bathroom, but those sounds just made me curious. I was already horny after seeing Cindy. *What would happen if I turned this doorknob?* There was nobody guarding the door, so what kind of VIP room was this really? I felt a little urine trickle out. I did a quick squeeze and held it in.

On the door there was a small little window. I could see a red dim light seeping through at the bottom of it. I had to get on my tippy toes to peek in. Whatever they had covering it was starting to peel away. *Oh, shit!* There were whips, belts, spiky shit tacked on the back walls. I squinted my eyes a bit then saw the naked bitch hanging from the ceiling like a puppet enjoying both men and women licking, fucking. It was tempting, truthfully.

The woman hung there hungry for the touch of everyone around her. From what I could make out, there were two guys and three girls. I had no idea how she was rigged, but it looked intense. It seemed like each person had control of her. All four of them were twisting and turning her into positions I had only seen in Kama Sutra books. They controlled how wide she spread her legs to how low she was to the floor. She had both dudes fucking her: one stroking deep into her flesh while the other guy used her mouth in the same manner. Her deep throat was no joke after seeing how far back her head was. The two girls kept themselves busy by sucking on her nipples and playing with their clits. I could see the two girls starting to twist their hands securing a rope. Then I saw the hanging woman's knees bending toward her chest. The dude fucking her didn't skip a beat either; he was still stroking while they was pulling her legs back.

Suddenly I felt a light hand on my back and a soft voice whispering into my ear: "Would you like to join?"

I damn near pissed myself I was so fucking scared. I stood against the door for a moment to catch my breath.

"Can you back up?" I scanned the scantily dressed female in front of me. I moved swiftly so my back wasn't against the door anymore. "It ain't that type a party. I'm just here supporting my friend," I said hastily.

"Do you want a closer look? I can get you in there."

"No. I was actually headed to the bathroom." I tried to go around her and bypass her offer.

"C'mon, you know you want a closer look. I'ma let you in free of charge only if you promise me you'll come back for a taste," she said smiling.

Oh, my God, did she actually suggest that like I was some stupid bitch? Damn, her game is weak. "Listen, like I said it ain't that type of party."

"Yeah, okay, I bet money that if I didn't touch you when I did yo' ass would've been rubbin' yo' pussy by now. So, stop frontin'." Her grin showed her true pimp game.

She wasn't wrong or right, but I wasn't about to do no dumb shit. "It's all good. I know you got to sell something in order to get it. I get it, you looking for next chick to hang from that ceiling. It ain't me." I arched my eyebrows and stood back waiting for her reaction.

"A'ight, shorty. Calm it down, ain't nobody tryin'a force you into nothin'." There she went flaunting those gold teeth again. It was corny.

I brushed past her and walked into the bathroom. I almost slammed the door against someone. There was a line. *When the fuck did all these bitches get here?*

After waiting for what seemed like forever I finally got into a stall to relieve myself. But if I'd known that I had to hold the door I would've pissed in the alley next door. Shit, I was already holding my pocketbook with my teeth, tissue paper in one hand, holding on to the broken lock with the other, and hovering over the toilet hoping that my dress didn't get splashed on.

This strip spot was crazy and I just wanted to get out of there. Cindy was just gonna have to understand that I couldn't stay around there until she was done. I headed out the bathroom and back to the bar. She wasn't on the stage anymore so I waited until she came out onto the floor for the up-close-and-personal lap dances. I didn't bother to order another drink. I couldn't dare go past that VIP room without another peek if I had to pee again.

Five minutes passed. No Cindy. Ten minutes passed. Still no Cindy. *Where the fuck could this bitch be?* I pulled my phone out to call her. I knew it might have been a stupid idea 'cause she wouldn't be walking around with her phone, but maybe she was getting dressed to come back out or something.

2 missed calls.

I was surprised to see she tried calling me, and then a text message popped up on the screen.

I'm out front. Come now.

This bitch out front; she can't be serious. She must be crazy. Doesn't she know all these horny-ass niggas got money to throw at her ass just to get a little closer? I hurried outside to see what her problem was. I thought she was there to make money.

When I saw her standing there smoking a cigarette that's when I knew something was wrong. She never smoked unless she was stressed or drinking. "Cindy, what happened?"

"Why you ain't tell me 'bout Big Red?" she asked with a snappy tone.

"What? Who the fuck is Big Red?" I honestly had no idea who she was talking about.

"Sherry, I swear to God I will beat yo' ass right here. Don't play dumb with me."

"Look here, I'm 'bout tired of you snapping at my ass. So either you gonna talk straight up or keep playing with fire. You do know what happens when you play with fire, right?" She wasn't going to speak to me in that manner without a warning.

"So you mean to tell me that you don't know some big red-headed bitch up in there?" She pointed to the building behind us.

"I already told you, no. Can you just tell me what happened?" I wished she would just say something instead of insisting on who I knew in there. Shit, I definitely didn't want to know nobody in there.

"That bitch tried to shake me down!" Her voice was loud.

I laughed. Cindy pushed me then flicked her cigarette my way. I shifted to the side quickly. "What the fuck!"

"Why the fuck you laughin'?" Cindy was madder now. I knew she didn't want to throw down in front of a strip club.

"C'mon, you can't tell me that ain't funny. How much money did you give her?"

"Bitch, did you forget where I'm from? I ain't give that big Amazon-lookin'-ass trick shit! She wasn't gonna make me give up my money like that. She tried to say that ain't no one school me on how she gets a percentage of what I make. That queen bee shit don't flow with me. I'm the only one runnin' my shit! Just 'cause I'm fresh and new to the game don't mean I ain't gonna keep what's mine. She just knew my money was cutting into her dollars for the night. She must be out her mind." Cindy pulled out another cigarette.

"Okay, so why you out here with yo' bags and shit? She must have put some fear into yo' ass if you standing in front of the strip club instead of inside making yo' money. I thought that's why you were here. Shit, I almost got put into a room and hung from the ceiling for a price. Don't tell me I dragged my ass over here to support you and yo' ass backin' out." She was a punk.

"Bitch, why don't you get up there and shake yo' ass! And where the fuck is Wayne? I sent him a text right after I texted you. I know he's here."

"Oh, please, that motherfucker ain't worried 'bout you. He too busy tryin'a work his way into a free lap dance from some stupid ho in there."

Cindy laughed loudly.

"So what you tryin'a do? You goin' in there or not?"

Cindy took a long drag off her cigarette. She looked up to the sky blowing the smoke out her lungs. "I got a betta plan, but I'm gonna need some help. You down?"

"What the fuck you talkin' about?" My eyebrows arched.

"Bitch, are you down or not? You gonna have to quit that fraud shit you doin' though."

Cindy looked like a light bulb lit in her head and she was going to do everything to keep it on. She didn't bother to wait for my response. "C'mon let's go. We got some work to do."

Wayne

3

Two weeks later . . .

"Cindy, stop playing and let me in. This shit is for the birds. I ain't tryin'a stay at my mom's no more. Besides you still got most of my shit in this bitch!" I banged at the door again, hoping she felt a little sorry for kicking my ass out.

There was no movement heard behind the door. I put my ear to the door. Still nothing.

"I know you home. I'ma stay out here until you open this fuckin' door. And I hope I see 'em nosey-ass neighbors, too. They gonna know all yo' business."

Suddenly I heard the deadbolt unlatch. *I knew she don't want her business out there like that.*

The door opened. There she stood fine as ever—flawless. "Wayne, I already told yo' ass I don't want to see yo' face. So why are you here?"

"C'mon, baby, I can't stay away. I thought we talked about this a week ago. What's up?"

"Ain't nothing up. From the way I see it you fucked up and yo' shit is packed and ready to go. Do you need me to call someone for you?" She folded her arms across her chest waiting for my answer.

I tried to move closer but she stepped out and closed the door behind her. "So, it's like that now? You can't forgive me?" I flashed those puppy dog eyes and inched my way into her personal space.

She stepped back quickly, causing her back to hit the door. Her reflexes kicked in and her hand stretched out to stop me from getting any closer. "Wayne, back the fuck up!"

"Who the fuck you think you talkin' to? I ought to slap the shit outta you for that. Stop playin' this stupid fuckin' game and let me in my house." This bitch got some nerve, like I didn't have a key. Shoving her little fine ass to the side, I reached into my pocket and pulled out my key. I heard her laughing.

"Have fun tryin'a get in. You forget I'm the one on the lease." She stood there with a grin on her face.

"So what, that shit don't mean nothin'."

"A'ight, then let me make a phone call." She pulled her cell out her back pocket and touched the screen. "Yes, I'm at 619 Sterling Place and my ex-boyfriend is tryin'a break into my house. I think he has a gun," she said loudly.

I saw the hatred in her eyes. She was taking it too far now. I snatched the phone out her hand and tossed it into the street.

"You fuckin' asshole! Why would you do that?" She darted down the steps of the brownstone only to see her phone in pieces on the pavement. "Oh, okay you want to play like that." Suddenly she smacked her own face and scratched her neck. She walked back. "Yo' ass goin' to jail, motherfucker."

Sirens sounded in the distance.

"You stupid-ass bitch," I shouted, heading down the steps, then spat into her face once I got close.

"You nasty motherfucker." She wiped her face. "You gonna pay for that shit," she hollered as I ran around the corner and slipped into the nearby project buildings. Those rookie cops wouldn't search Albany Projects anytime soon for one guy with a gun when everybody in there holding something.

I didn't believe she could do that to me after all the shit we been through. *Fuck, what the hell am I gonna do now?* I thought as I walked through the projects. I kept walking and ended up in the Stuy at my man's house. I sat on the sofa spilling my heartache like a bitch.

"Yo, she fuckin' called the cops in front of me, then after tossing her shit she smacked herself. And if that wasn't crazy enough she dug her long-ass nails into her neck so a mark would be there once those fools showed up."

Aaron laughed at my ass. "You's a stupid-ass nigga. Why the fuck you go over there? You ain't seen her ass for at least a week that I know of."

"Nigga, I just fucked her two nights ago over at Sherry's crib on Nostrand. I thought we was good."

"You still the fool. Did you call her after you fucked her? I'm guessing no, yo' ass just show up a couple days later at her door—"

"She ain't pay no fuckin' rent. I do, nigga. I'm the one in these streets riskin' everything to put a fuckin' roof over her head." I had to set him straight.

"A'ight, a'ight, calm the fuck down. I ain't call the pigs on you. C'mon, my cousin Rich on Putnam having a little something. He got drinks, food, chicks, and weed. Let's go clear yo' mind."

"Yeah, I'm down with that."

After a few drinks and an abundance of high-grade chronic, my mood changed for the better. The sounds of Beres Hammond thumping from the speaker boxes made me forget about the day until I spotted Sherry.

I tapped hard on Aaron's shoulder. "Yo, Aaron, how the fuck Sherry here?"

"How you mean? She the one providing the liqs. Now don't go over there and start no shit. I ain't tryin'a break up no fight. I'm drunk and high," he slurred out.

"Well, that means that Cindy 'round somewhere."

"So what if she is? Go grind on one of 'em young ones over there. They look like they ready . . ." He swayed over to the crowd of girls, moving his hips like a drunken old man.

That's when I saw her—the prettiest girl there: Cindy. I wanted to run up to her and plant a big juicy kiss on her soft lips, but I knew that wasn't a possibility. I just stood there alone. I watched her sip on her Heineken bottle through a straw. Her hair was down around her face, probably to hide what she did earlier. Her white shorts were short and tight, just the way I liked it: showing enough ass to tease. Cindy's body was any man's dream: her round, perky breasts, small waist, and a juicy ass that made my mouth water.

With the music blaring and her standing there with the street light hitting her made me think back to the time when she knew nothing. I was the one who taught her everything: sex, kissing, sucking, even scheming on other niggas. I had to say something. I couldn't let her just stand there; besides I kinda knew all these niggas was gonna try to get at her eventually. I wanted to make sure I could still get it.

When I was headed her way I saw some short, stocky dude chatting her up. Her smiles looked flirty. Aaron was still tryin' to grind his way into the girls' dancing circle. I stood there watching her interact with this dude. I didn't like it. I started grinding my teeth and my high left instantly. He started to grind on her, but she shoved him away. He pulled on her hand forcing her closer to him. I couldn't stand there and let that go down. I walked over there calmly.

"Yo, my man, I don't think she wanna dance." He still had his grip on her. "Let her go!" My voice was loud now.

"Why don't you mind yo' business," he offered.

"Nah, homie, you should." At that moment I punched him dead center on the chin. He hit the ground like a toppling tree.

"Now why you do that?" Cindy asked with a smile.

"I didn't like his hands on you. I'm sorry, baby."

Everyone surrounded the stiff body on the ground and of course laughter was heard when the drunkest person yelled out the famous line, "You got knocked the fuck out."

I grabbed my baby into my arms and pleaded how sorry I was for the way I acted. She didn't resist so I knew there was an opportunity for the taking. I whispered in her ear, "I love you, forever, baby. Please take me back. I miss you."

"I love you too. Let me tell Sherry I'm leavin'." She never let go of my hand as we walked over to the make-shift bar. "Sherry, I'm leavin' with Wayne. See what you can do here."

Sherry's jaw dropped after hearing Wayne's name. After an awkward silence she finally asked, "You ain't serious?"

"Girl, don't trip. Besides you one suggested we start here. So it was meant to be. Call me tomorrow, we'll talk."

"Girl, I hope you know what you doin'." Sherry looked to me. "Wayne, don't think you okay in my book. 'Cause you best to believe if you would've—"

"Sherry, I already told you I got this, fall back," Cindy said with confidence.

"Okay, then I guess I'll talk to you later."

I walked away hand in hand with my lady by my side. *I got her back. I'm gonna fuck the shit outta her once we get home. She's never gonna be able to let me go.*

Sherry

4

The music died down. It was four in the morning and bitches were still hanging around hoping to hook some fat pockets. Most of the night, I was setting up the play for Cindy to do all the interaction, not me, feeding them drinks and weed. *Now I got to do this shit solo. Ain't this a bitch! Cindy gonna get a piece of my mind when I see her ass.*

This was supposed to go smooth. I get them feeling good and Cindy would be there chatting them up, feeling them out. *I better make something happen since Cindy left me high and dry.*

"Damn, I wanna go to the diner. Who comin'?" I said out loud to see who was listening.

"Me . . ." a drunk, loud voice said.

"Aaron, you can't even walk, let alone order a meal. Go lay yo' head somewhere. What 'bout y'all?" I looked over to the ladies surrounding Aaron. I knew that look on their faces—*they broke as hell and don't have a pot to piss in.* I figured I needed to assure them, "Don't worry, I got it. I just need somebody to drive."

"I'll drive. Let's go," Rich said pumping his fist in the air.

That was perfect; he was helping me out and didn't even know it. "C'mon, y'all, only four can fit in his ride and there's four of you standing here. There's only two seats open so who's goin'?"

It was funny to see their faces now. Each of them giving the evil eye to one another, then trying to pull rank on each other.

"Bitch, I copped yo' outfit to come here. I'm goin'," one of the girls muffled to the other.

I almost laughed out loud when I heard that. *This just might be that easy.* I sure as hell didn't want anyone to break out into a fight just for some cheap breakfast. So I did the only thing any man in my position would have done—picked the baddest two chicks and headed to the car.

"I ain't wanna go wit' y'all anyway," one of the chicks said, trying to keep Aaron balanced. *Someone should really tell her just 'cause you show everything don't mean you get everything.*

Rich pulled into the parking lot of Mike's Diner on Utica Avenue, near Winthrop Street, and parked. There were a lot of cars. *Damn, it had to be crowded.* I got out the car and pulled the passenger front seat up to let the girls out. I hated his little fucking Honda Accord; it had no space. He made enough money to get something nice. He was just a cheap ass. But I got no right to talk, 'cause I ain't got shit—at least not yet. The girls weren't talkative in the car at all. They just sat back. Shit, I didn't even know their names. *Oh, my God, Cindy is so much better at this shit.*

We walked up to the entrance; the girls were behind us. The girls looked around when we entered like they didn't want to run into anyone they knew. The hostess got us seated and handed us menus.

"Can I get anyone coffee or tea?" the waitress asked.

"Nah, no coffee for me. Can I have some orange juice instead?" one of the girls responded.

"I'll take a glass too, thanks," I added.

"Do you guys make lattes?" the other girl asked.

"Latte? Well, ain't we a Starbuck's lover," I said causing everyone to chuckle including the waitress.

After the waitress brought us our drinks we placed our orders. While we were waiting I had to ask, "Hey, what y'all names anyway?"

They both laughed.

"I'm Stacie and she's Diamond."

Rich got up suddenly and walked over to another table. I didn't know who the guys were, but I was happy for the chance to be alone with the girls. "So, y'all over eighteen right?"

They both looked at each other.

"Yeah, why?" Stacie asked.

"Nah, 'cause I don't need nobody's mamas hunting y'all down," I joked.

"You funny, so who yo' man?" Diamond asked.

"My man? It sure as hell ain't Rich if that's what you was thinking."

"Good, so he up for the picking, huh?" Stacie's brow arched.

"What you want with Rich? He ain't got nothin' you want. He a average nigga, nothin' spectacular," I said in a low voice, looking over at Rich still talking to his boys at the other table.

"Average is good. It's stable. You don't have to worry 'bout jealous niggas wanting what you got," Diamond said taking a sip of orange juice.

That was new. This chick might be a little difficult to convince, but I had try anyway. I eased the conversation in a different direction. "So, what y'all do for money?"

Stacie answered quickly, "We do what we have to."

"Well, that could mean damn near anything. Don't tell me y'all selling ass too." I suggested the obvious.

"Wait, hold up; what is this shit anyway? It sounds like you want to be a pimp. Yo, Diamond, I think we gots to go. This was a setup. She already know what we do. Let's bounce." Stacie stood up.

"Shit, I'm fucking starving. You can go," Diamond said watching the waitress placing the plates on the table.

"Okay, here you go. Enjoy, just let me know if you need anything else, all right?" the waitress said.

"Listen, ain't nobody tryin'a pimp nobody. Y'all too smart for that shit. Just sit down and eat yo' food." I hollered at Rich to come eat his food before it got cold. Ain't nothing worse than cold eggs.

All I thought of was how Cindy was going to kill me since I blew this opportunity. *Her ass shoulda been here to do her part.*

We all ate in awkward silence.

After eating, we all piled into the car and Rich asked, "Where y'all stayin' at?"

"Albany Projects," Diamond answered.

"A'ight then." Rich started the car and drove out the parking lot.

Well, this was a bust. What was I thinking? How can I recruit girls if I don't know how to do it? "Yo, Rich, drop me at Cindy's," I insisted.

Cindy

5

A loud buzzing sounded off. Whoever it was kept their finger on it, causing a continuous noise. I was sure it wasn't just me being woken up this early.

"Yo, who the fuck is that? It's like six in the morning," Wayne shouted from the bathroom as he relieved himself.

"Oh, shut up. Just go answer the door. I got to put some clothes on," I said climbing out the bed. Wayne slapped my ass as he walked out the room.

Soon the buzzing stopped and a few seconds after I heard the door open. Sherry's voice hollered out, "Where Cindy at?"

"Damn . . . no hello. What kinda shit is that? You in my house, you know," Wayne replied after slamming the door shut.

"Nigga, please, go take yo' whack ass somewhere. Cindy, where you at?" Sherry hollered.

"I'm here, I'm here." I rushed into the living room. "Y'all need to stop that shit especially if *you* tryin'a help, Wayne." I just stood there with my arms folded across my chest.

"Wait, hold up, what the fuck you mean help? You told him what we doin'?" Sherry asked confused.

"Sherry, don't," I quickly said.

"Yeah, Sherry, I know what y'all tryin'a to do so play yo' role," Wayne imposed his position.

"I thought you was gonna take a shower. Me and Sherry need to talk."

"Yeah, a'ight, you betta set her straight," he said walking toward the bathroom.

The look on Sherry's face said it all—if she had a knife she would have stabbed him in the neck and left him for dead with no remorse.

"Cindy, what the fuck are you really doin'? 'Cause that nigga ain't gonna be talkin' to me like that. He can talk to you that way, but he gonna get a rude awakening doin' that shit to me." Sherry wasn't happy.

"Listen, he's only candy for the girls we need. Do you think I'm gonna be taking these calls when they really start poppin'? Since I put this nine-hundred number out there I've been the only one tryin' to make this work. Now, what happened at the party?"

Sherry knew I was right. Ever since I put some ads out in the *Village Voice* and local sex shops, the calls weren't coming in as I anticipated. It definitely didn't help that once they found out meeting for a price was only a fantasy. This phone sex service wasn't as easy as I thought. I only hoped Sherry had better news for me.

"Those girls weren't doin' shit. They weren't desperate enough."

"But I thought you said that party held nothin' but lazy hoes. So you mean to tell me you ain't even get a number from a chick?" I asked annoyed.

Sherry rolled her eyes. "Maybe if you was there, you would've been there to do what was needed. I don't know nothin' about this shit. I ain't no pimp or ho, let's get that straight." She folded her arms on her chest and leaned against the back of the leather recliner.

"You right, I should have been there."

"Yeah, you had to get yo' pussy licked and smashed so you wasn't thinkin' 'bout shit. Look, this recruiting chicks ain't my skill so come up with somethin' better. Now what?"

Sherry wasn't wrong, but she wasn't right either 'cause if this was going to work she had to do everything needed to make this money. "Okay, maybe we just comin' at this shit all wrong. I was doing some research and come to find out Web cams was the new wave of phone sex without the phone." I waited to see her reaction.

"Web cam?" Sherry's lip curled up.

"You heard me." I walked over to the hallway entrance so I could hear if the shower was still running. Sherry finally took a seat on the sofa. I hurried back to the living room and took a seat next to her.

"Who the hell gonna be in front of the camera?" she asked in a low voice.

"Well, that's what I wanted to talk to you 'bout." I had to be delicate before Sherry cussed my ass out. "I was thinking that for now maybe—"

"Oh, hell no." Sherry stood up and her voice got louder. "Here you are tryin'a pimp my ass but yet I'm supposed to be yo' fuckin' partner. What the fuck!"

If I wanted her to be all in then I had to be all in. "Would you listen and stop actin' like that. *You are my partner,* but if we really want this we gotta get dirty, too."

"Are you sayin' what I think you sayin'?" Sherry pulled her head back and tilted it to the side. "And where or when do you think this is happenin'?"

"Since money is short and yo' ass sure ain't putting nothin' in the pot, I think we should do it here." I swallowed hard trying not to give away my hesitance.

"So, you okay with just putting yo' face all out there like that?"

"Well, not exactly. I was thinking that we could wear those masquerade ballroom masks. You know, the ones that just cover yo' eyes." It really didn't sound good when I said it out loud.

"I think you need to get rid of Wayne so we could really talk about this shit. I can't stand his ass. And why would you—"

"I think we can save that conversation for another day. Here he comes," I interrupted.

"What y'all two talkin' 'bout?"

I looked at him—no, matter of fact, I stared at his ass. He was clean shaven, smelling good, tight plain white T-shirt on showing off his elaborate tattoos on his muscular arms. His jeans fit him perfectly on his waist, not tight like skater boys or hanging off his ass. "Where you goin'?" I tilted my head waiting for his answer.

"Nah, I got somethin' with Kev. You know him, right? He got this photo shoot for Viva La Brooklyn. I'ma meet him over there." He looked at his watch. "Shit, I was supposed to be there already." I could see him inching toward the door as if his answer was sufficient.

My leg was shaking; I was pissed. After all that shit he said last night. How he was going to change and put an effort into this relationship. I fell for it. I hated him more at that moment than ever. I knew he wasn't going to a photo shoot. Most likely he was taking somebody to breakfast before they had to go to work; it was a weekday. He was trying to be sweet to someone. The more I thought about it, the more I wanted to dig into his ass.

"Photo shoot, huh, where at?"

"Yeah, you heard me."

There he goes with that tone. He always thinks he's so slick with his "I'ma get into an argument first" shit. He wanted to be guilt free of the dirt he was about to roll around with.

"Since you late already, just wait for me. I'm coming." I stood up and headed to the bedroom. I quickly threw on some jeans and a tank top and headed back into the living room.

Wayne was already approaching the door by the time I returned.

"You can't go like that. Yo' hair all over the place, and yo' tracks showin'. You got no makeup on; you look a hot mess. Besides it's gonna take you too long to get yo'self lookin' right. I'm late as is."

Sherry busted out laughing. "And he yo' man," she added.

"You know what, why don't you both shut the hell up! And, you"—I pointed at Wayne—"if you think that you can just fuck me and then go see some next bitch you got a fuckin' problem. You better not even show yo' ass over here later, bye!" I walked in front of him and opened the door for him.

"You's a fuckin' bitch!" He walked out with ease and I slammed the door behind him.

"Fuck him. I told you he ain't shit. Why you still fuckin' him? Is the dick really that good to be treated like that?" Sherry just had to put her two cents in; she was asking the right questions, too.

My mind was spinning. I couldn't believe after all the shit we talked about he was still going to be the dog I learned he was. That's it, it was over. I made up my mind.

"Sherry, what the fuck do you know about even having a man? I have known you for years now and I still ain't never seen you with a man for more than a week. So please, I don't need yo' input when you have little to no experience with relationships."

I didn't care if she was right. She never had any real relationship. It was always a fling or a one-night stand. If she was going to give me advice she better get a man for more than a few weeks.

"You know what, Cindy, I think I better leave. Maybe you should think 'bout what I just did to help you start this bullshit sex line. I done stopped fucking with the credit card shit, thinking this was gonna bring me enough to cover my needs and style, but if you expect me to do—"

"First of all, I didn't make you do nothin'. I posed an idea to you and you agreed. Let's get that straight. Second, that nigga, Wayne, ain't nobody business but mine. If you got a problem then you should walk now unless you fuckin' him too. Third, you conveniently forgot that I've been the one answerin' calls not you. So you should think before you start poppin' off at the mouth." I took a seat back on the sofa. I could see her anger rising within, but she knew I was right.

"A'ight, Cindy, if you want me out this shit then say so. I can easily get back to credit card fraud."

"What?" My voice got loud. "So you gonna go back to some bullshit that you can do some real time for?"

"Fuck you and that lame-ass nigga you with. 'Cause I ain't tryin' to beg nobody for shit." Sherry's face showed her seriousness.

"Look, I ain't tryin'a fuckin' fight with yo' ass 'cause of that lame-ass nigga Wayne. Look, all I know is I can't do this shit by myself and you supposed to be my girl. My ride or die chick. Now 'cause of Wayne you actin' like you don't want to make money. Are you in or out? That's all I need to know, on some real shit." I waited patiently while she fidgeted on the sofa.

Sherry didn't agree or disagree. She pulled her phone out and punched at the screen then showed it to me. It was Craigslist. I looked at her confused.

"If we put the sex line on this shit I'm sure we can make some money."

I smiled. She was willing to make it work even if that meant that Wayne was around. If he needed to think I was his girl in order to receive his help then I'd do it.

I had to make this work. I wanted the money and the legitimacy. I knew Sherry did too. I wanted to be bigger than what I was.

Wayne

6

A week later . . .

"Oh, my God. Heaven finally answered my prayers. They sent me my angel." I tried my best to woo her.

"Wayne, you sure know what to say to a girl, don't you?" Sherry rolled her eyes.

If only she knew how good her ass looked when she turned around. I knew it ain't right, but since me and Cindy got back together she'd been around a lot—too much for me not to notice.

"So, what you want me to do, Cindy?"

"What you do best, of course. I need you to go get some girls so we can get this money. Are you with it?" Cindy asked like she didn't already know the answer.

"Damn straight. I already got two chicks willing to do anything for me," I said testing my boundaries with her.

"Okay, well where they at?"

I was a bit surprised at her question. I looked at her; she was calm. There was no animosity, no jealous attitude, just hungry for the future. That was a good sign and every inch she allowed I took. *Slowly but surely I'll be in control and she won't know what hit her,* my mind wandered.

"Is there a problem with yo' phone?" Sherry asked.

I turned to Sherry. "Nah, why?" I shrugged.

"For someone who got two chicks waiting in the wings and willing to do whateva, it sure is takin' you mighty long to get this money." Sherry always had to open her mouth to stir some shit up.

"Sherry, you really need to stop. A'ight, give me an hour." I stood up and headed toward the door.

"Wait, where you goin'?" Cindy asked.

I turned around and answered, "I gotta go get 'em. I can't just make a call."

"Why not?" Sherry chimed in.

There she go with her shit. "'Cause this pimpin' shit don't work like that. That's why. Now either y'all want these girls or not. Cindy, we already spoke 'bout this. I don't love these hoes. This is just business and you know how shit might have to go down." I turned toward the door and let myself out without another word.

I walked out the house with a smile on my face. If I played my cards right this might become my lifelong fantasy since I busted my first nut. Now, the way I saw it my dirt wasn't so dirty since I was the one getting the product.

Two hours later . . .

"Damn, baby, why haven't I seen you? I miss you." She kissed me on my neck. "C'mon, baby, where's my lovin' at? You know I need it."

"We gotta talk before we get all into that." I walked past her and sat on the chaise in the living room. Dee knelt in front of me.

"I don't like the sound of that," She started to unbuckle my pants and eased her warm hand against the opening of my boxers.

It felt so good. I didn't want her to stop, but I needed her to. I had some serious plans for us. The more I delayed stopping her, the harder my dick became. I allowed her to rub my dick a little.

"Y'know you want it, daddy," she whispered.

"Stop talking . . . put it in yo' mouth . . ."

She pulled my pants down to my ankles and pulled my cock through the slit of my boxers. Her soft lips slowly glided up and down my ten-inch shaft.

"Mmm . . . don't tease me like that . . . show daddy what you got." My mind was at ease and in complete bliss when she swallowed all of me. Her deep throat was no joke; it was even better when I stood.

"Ahh yeah, daddy, make it harder for me, daddy." She slapped my stiff cock against her cheek and jerked me faster.

"Yes . . . you like my big dick in yo' mouth . . . yeah, that's it . . . suck it."

I watched as my dick disappeared deeper into her dripping mouth. I could feel my climax reaching quickly. I reached out and held her face still so I could fuck her mouth like a blow-up doll. I could feel the back of her throat tightening on my head. She was doing her best not to gag. But the way I was ramming her face down on my jimmy there was nothing else left for her to do; she had to wait until I was done.

"Daaammmnnnn . . ." I let out, still keeping her face in position.

I could feel her gentle taps on my thighs trying to convey me to release my grip. I didn't want to, but I did eventually.

"You feel good, daddy?"

"I feel okay." I stroked my manhood still at attention.

"I see you ready for me now. Y'know me, I don't like that first nut. It's always too fast. Let's take it to the bedroom and have some real fun," Dee said smiling as she rose to her feet.

I immediately kicked off my sneakers, pulled my pants off along with my boxers, and my T-shirt. I looked at my phone lying on the floor. The notification light was flashing. I forgot my phone was on silent. I picked it up and swiped my password in.

> 3 missed calls
> 2 voice mails
> 5 new text messages

I checked my voice mail; there was no surprise when I heard Cindy's voice. My dick went limp noodle instantly. I didn't bother to listen to the entire message. I just exited out of my voice mails and put my phone into sleep mode.

"Daddy, what . . ." She saw me holding my phone. "Who you talkin' to? It's that bitch, isn't it? I shoulda smacked her ass when I saw you with her. You said you wasn't fuckin' with her no more."

"I know . . . but that's what I had to talk to you 'bout." I took a seat on the edge of the sofa then continued, "You see, Cindy got somethin' goin' and I have to be a part of it in order to get this money for us."

"What she got goin' on? What, she know some people for you to rob?" Dee chuckled walking toward the sofa.

I felt insulted. I lunged for her and pulled her down to the floor then got on top of her. I pushed her hands above her head and got in her face. "Who the fuck you think you talkin' to, bitch? And who the fuck you laughin' at?"

Dee's eyes widened and her fear was obvious. I didn't have to hit her, nor did I want to. I wanted her to know she wasn't going to get away with that slick shit. She hit a nerve and pushed a button at the same time.

"I wasn't laughing at you." Her bottom lip trembled a bit and her eyes started to water.

I let my grip go and got off her. "Next time watch what you say."

"I'm sorry, daddy," she said in a low voice.

"I hate when you make me do you like that. I don't want to hit you, but you be pushin' me to that edge. I hate that shit." I got up from the floor and put my boxers and pants on. I snatched the phone off the sofa and put in my pocket. I had to play this right.

"Don't leave. I'm not mad. Please don't leave. Tell me what you was gonna say. Let's just forget about what just happened." She tried to delay me with words; it was cute.

"Listen, I thought you was okay with me fuckin' other people as long as I come back to you. What the fuck is yo' problem? I thought we had an understandin'.'" I took a seat on the sofa and bowed my head like I had a headache.

Dee sat next to me and put her arm around me, "Daddy, I know but sometimes I just can't bear the thought that you might not come back to me. I haven't seen you since the block party. I love you so much. I would do anything for you. You know that, right?"

"You wouldn't do anything for me." I raised my head and stared into her eyes.

"Yes, I would. I'm already dancin' like you asked me to get some extra paper on the side."

"Wait hold up, I didn't ask you to do shit. You was the one cryin' 'bout all the shit you don't have, a'ight? Don't blame me for the shit you wanted to do in the first place." I saw her wiggling a bit like she wanted to tell me something, but was scared now after what I just did and said. Well, I was about to find out either way.

"Remember when you said if an opportunity knocks and it's enough money that I shouldn't let what we got hold me back? Well, last night I went to this new club in Queens." She paused and stared at my fists. After a minute she continued, "This old, wrinkled man walked in and offered me a band to play with his balls while he fondled my nipples." She inched away a little. "I did it." Her smile showed how proud she was.

"What you did with the money?" I asked since this was the first time she actually did something. She'd been dancing for about two months and from day one I was pushing her to trick on the side.

"I bought you a little somethin'-somethin', daddy."

"What?" I gestured my hands open.

Dee hurried into the bedroom and returned holding a small white bag with black printed Gucci symbols on it. She handed it to me with a huge smile across her face.

"That's a mighty small bag . . ."

"Here, daddy, I thought these would fit you. Go 'head, look in the bag. Tell me how much you love them."

I reached into the bag and pulled out a wad of tissue paper. I was disappointed once I saw that it was sunglasses. *What the fuck I need another pair of sunglasses for?* This was nice, but I would've rather she just gave me the cash. "Thanks," I forced out with a smile.

"What's the matter, you don't like 'em?"

"Nah, it ain't that." I kissed her on the lips softly. "It's just that I could've used the cash that's all. I need to hire somebody to do some videos for me and I was hoping you would help me out with that." I hoped she packed the receipt in the bag. I grabbed the bag and looked in it; there was nothing but more tissue paper.

"I got the receipt in my purse. I'll take it back and call you when I have the cash," she said in a whiny voice.

I hated that tone she used when something didn't go the way she planned it. I was sure she expected me to show her love because they were Gucci, but that was so beneath me. All she wanted from me was attention and she thought giving me expensive gifts would keep me around. If only she knew the only thing that would keep me around was her in front of a camera.

"Don't worry 'bout it, daddy. Listen, I got a new toy." She smoothly nestled herself into my lap.

I mumbled, "Another one?" Her toys scared me on some real shit. I remembered the first night I fucked her she pulled out one of those clear glass dildos and wanted me to stick it in her ass while I ate her out. Her look of displeasure when she found out that I didn't eat nobody else's pussy but my wifey's was priceless. But I made it up to her that night without going back on my words; I invited her friend into our bed for our second go-around.

"C'mon, don't'cha wanna play?" Dee's voice sounded a little annoyed.

There was a gentle pulse beginning to erupt in my smaller head. I grabbed my phone. "I'll play with you only if you let me record it."

Her eyes lit up and her pearly whites were shining. "Daddy, you can do whateva you want."

I held my phone out in front of me. She spun around and twerked for the camera immediately. Dee's round bubble ass jiggled and clapped like a pro. *This is gonna be easier than I thought. I don't gotta tell this bitch nothin', just dick her ass down on the regular. I'll just have to keep Cindy busy, but I think I got an idea. If I get another chick or two, that should keep her busy.*

I got so lost in my thoughts that I didn't even realize my dick wasn't up to bat anymore and my camera wasn't focused on Dee either.

"Daddy . . . " She stood up realizing my focus was off.

I caught myself before she started to question me about my thoughts. "C'mon, baby, let's take this in the room. There's some tricks I want you to show the camera."

"Yes, daddy, that's what I want to hear. Let's go, I'm ready," she said walking into the bedroom.

Sherry

7

This was the type of shit that had me on edge—the unknown. Wayne left three hours ago and he wasn't back yet. *Cindy better know what she's fucking doing.* Letting her man walk out of here and knowingly allow him to bring back some random hoes to *her* house was a bold move. I didn't know who had more balls, him or her.

Sitting at the kitchen table waiting for Wayne to return was making me worry about the future. I knew Cindy was about getting money, but I wasn't about to pimp nobody. I just only hoped she knew that about me. "Yo, Cindy, do you think he's comin' back?"

"His ass better come back and it better not be empty-handed." Cindy did her best to hide her worried look with sharp words.

"Are you really tryin'a pimp these hoes? Is that your game plan?"

She laughed at me. "Sherry, do I look like a pimp?"

"Shit, I don't know anymore. The way you pressin' on Wayne for 'em hoes I don't know what your main plan is. I know the end plan is to get money, but we gotta have it set up right so these girls don't act out on either one of our asses. Shit, I ain't going jail over no bullshit, trust me."

"I'm pressin' Wayne 'cause yo' ass won't do it. I'ma call his ass again. If he don't pick up I'ma—"

I heard the front door open, but only heard one pair of footsteps. "I told you he sucks," I said hitting her with the "I told you so" look as well. I sat back and watched the show; it just might get physical and that would give me cause to beat his ass like I really wanted to.

"Wayne, where the fuck you been?" Cindy got in his face real quick at the door.

"C'mon now I don't need all that." He threw his hands up like a stop sign. "You calm yo' self down. After I show you what I got here, you gonna love me." He walked over to the sofa and pulled out his phone.

I got up and stood near the sofa. Cindy swarmed in close to him and took a seat next to him. We both looked at each other and smirked.

"A'ight, this is who can make us some money on the level you talkin' 'bout." He swiped the phone screen and a video appeared. Those iPhone screens were so damn small I had to sit on the other side of him to get a better view.

"Who the hell is that?" Cindy shouted immediately.

"Just fuckin' watch the show and ask questions later," Wyane blurted out.

"Damn, she looks familiar," I said watching the skinny, tall, light-skinned young girl showing all her goods for the camera.

"No, she don't. She ain't even from around here," Wayne said giving me the "don't say nothin'" look. I couldn't place her face, but I knew he was lying through his teeth.

"So what we gonna do with this? She ain't here and you better not have her on the strip either. 'Cause that ain't gonna get us nowhere." Cindy made her point.

"Wayne, will this girl sign a release to use this video? That's what we need to happen."

"A release? Why the fuck we need that shit for some ho?" He laughed at me.

"We need something if you want your cut. Let's just say this bullshit-ass video actually puts us out there and we make some money. What happens when she accidently sees it? She gonna want part of the money, then what? You gonna pay lawyer fees, court fees, and whateva else that comes along with fightin' her ass right?" He was so fucking stupid. I had a feeling that this was just some side chick he got buying him shit and giving him pocket money. His slick ass got her to do something stupid and he wasn't even going to tell her his intentions with the video.

"Wayne, Sherry's right. You can't do shit like that. If that's yo' little jump-off then get her to sign a release form. Sherry, did you print any of those out we saw online?" Cindy asked with a bit of attitude.

I could tell Cindy was pissed at him; not only did he deliberately show her the video, but he'd forgotten that his voice was also recorded. All those "show daddy what you got" and "daddy wants you to" do this and that. I knew that wasn't easy for her to sit there and not react to it. She had to keep herself under control or Wayne would take her idea and run with it.

"Yeah, I printed out a few copies. It's still on the printer over there," I said pointing to the small side table across the room.

Cindy got up from the sofa and retrieved the papers off the printer. She handed a couple sheets to Wayne. "Go back and make her sign this then we can make this happen."

"What if she don't wanna sign it?"

"Then you tell her you gonna be in the videos too and sign one in front of her. Shit, you could make another cute little video if you want."

I almost choked on my own spit. Wayne's face looked more surprised, but I knew he wasn't going to pass up an open invitation. I quickly got up and headed to the kitchen to get a bottle of water. I couldn't believe I heard her say that. *She is gonna let him fuck other chicks and have that shit on camera. This bitch is nuts. I better get out while I can.* Thoughts flushed my mind. I couldn't figure out where her head was at. I stood by the fridge gulping down the bottle of water, turning my back toward them.

"Wait hold up, I never said I wanted to be in these videos," Wayne said defensively and loud.

"Lower your voice, ain't nobody trippin'. Don't you like to fuck?" Cindy stood in front of him and folded her arms across her chest.

"Baby, c'mon . . . what you sayin'?" Wayne sounded almost disappointed.

"Look it was just a suggestion, nothing to do with our personal status but our only business relationship. I'm sure you understand. Besides your big dick just might make us more money."

Cindy's words shocked me even more now. It seemed like she was trying to pimp him in a slick-ass way. I saw her waving the paper in his face.

"Get her to sign this shit and don't come back 'til you do." Cindy walked over to the front door and opened it for him. She pecked him on the lips when he approached the door and gave him a pat on his ass, sending him on his way.

Once she closed the door I asked the obvious: "Now you want to do porno flicks? And you want yo' fuckin' man in 'em? What the fuck is goin' on, Cindy? Are you fuckin' losin' it?" I was confused she never mentioned this shit. All she talked about was getting some stupid bitches to make some easy money over the phone.

She turned around with tears in her eyes—she was hurt. I felt bad for assaulting her with all the questions;

she didn't necessarily need that from me right now—she needed her friend. I walked over to her and just held her. I could feel her body off-balance. "Cindy, you better sit down. C'mon, I got you." I helped her to the sofa.

There were no words coming out her mouth; she was sobbing. After seating her on the sofa I walked into the bathroom and grabbed a box of tissues off the top of the toilet. I returned to the living room and she was now louder; her cries became yells.

"I knew that motherfucka couldn't be true to his word. All he does is fuckin' lie. Why would he do that to me? After all I've done for him. I ain't never snitched on his ass when cops was pressin' me 'bout his whereabouts. He ain't shit!" Cindy screamed.

Suddenly she stood up and started to pace the floor. I was a little scared at first, but then I watched her for a moment. It looked like motivation started to set in from her soldier-like march.

"Sherry, do you think you can go back to the strip club with me and show me that chick who approached you? You don't gotta say nothin'. I'll handle everything. We 'bout to get paid real quick. I'm through with this nigga. I swear!"

"Cindy . . . umm . . . wait, first you gotta tell me what you thinkin'. 'Cause right now I'm lost. I thought we were settin' up a phone sex line, not throwin' ourselves in the pimpin' business. Cindy, you my girl and everything, but I definitely ain't jumpin' into nothin' without knowing what's in the water. I spent my last on that LLC you made me get. Now I'm 'bout to move in here on some real shit."

"I got you, if you need to move in. You're the only one who really has my back."

I rolled my eyes at her. "Bitch, you know I ain't movin' in here as long as you got that asshole around. And what the fuck you know 'bout the porn industry?"

"Oh, there ain't much to it, trust me. Besides I got plans for his ass. Keeping Wayne busy and happy ain't gonna be hard. Pussy and money is what drives him so then we won't have to deal with his ass."

"And what exactly you gonna have him do?" I didn't believe her, although this time her tone had a little more sting to it. "You just gonna let his ass take over your life and he gonna do the same shit to you over and over again."

"Okay, I'll make a deal with you: come with me to the strip club so that we can start this shit off right and you can be my partner. Wayne won't be in charge of nothin' but his dick. I won't allow him back into my life like before."

"How can you say that? He ain't even worth having around. You just sayin' shit. Bitch, I ain't jumpin' off no cliff with you," I pushed.

"This time is different. He's not go—"

"Shut up, you sound like a domestic violence commercial. Stop actin' like you got this all figured out. Shit, ain't that simple," I snapped, growing tired of her forever promises about Wayne. I needed to get out and get out fast before I got in too deep and drowned with no one to save me. *She's my girl, but right now I got no money coming in because I thought she was real about her game. What the fuck is really goin' on?*

Cindy walked out of the room and returned with a huge envelope. "This is all I have. I've been stashin' since Wayne started his robbery spurts about six months ago."

My eyes widened when I saw all the cash stuffed into the manila envelope when she opened it. "Does he know you have this?" I looked back at the door real quick.

"I ain't that stupid. I've been takin' a little every time he handed me a bag of money to count. But now all that has stopped. Nowadays, he's just been givin' me some dollars here and there."

I pushed her hand back holding the envelope. I sat silent for a moment, confused. *First she loves him; then she wants him to help us but he won't be making any decisions.* I knew for a fact it wouldn't work out that way. *How the hell does that work?* I thought she felt my hesitation.

"Sherry, I know what you sayin'. Look, its different this time. He ain't gonna be runnin' nothin' on this end. Trust me."

I sunk back into the sofa, kicked off my pumps, and laid my head on the pillows. Sitting there in silence, I didn't know if I was just tired or she was really trying to convince me that she was in control. Cindy only knew one dick and that was Wayne. As much as I dragged her to every party, this concert, that event, and introduced her to a number of fine-ass brothers she never hooked up with none. It was so crazy to me the love she had for this man. I honestly didn't think I could love anyone that much. *She's so stupid,* I thought.

"You know I'm tired as hell. I need to catch some sleep then we can talk some more 'bout this. 'Cause, girl, you got me on stuck right now and I can't see or hear you straight."

"You can sleep when you dead. Look at it this way, if we let Wayne be Wayne we won't have to worry 'bout gettin' no girls. We just let him do all the work. Besides he's probably tickled pink that I ain't bitchin' with his ass 'bout that video." She laughed.

"Okay, you go 'head and laugh but I know that you feelin' some kinda way now that it's clear he's fuckin' other bitches without any care for you, as I've told yo' ass before." I stared at her waiting for her flow of tears.

"Like I ain't supposed to feel a way. C'mon now, Sherry, this was the man I was supposed to spend the rest of my life with. Now that he can't deny it or manipulate me anymore it's a entirely different game. Love is blind but I ain't tryin' to be blind anymore. I'm tired of living off his words 'I'm tryin' to make somethin' happen,' or how much he loves me and he had a moment of weakness. Or, his favorite line, 'I was drunk and high,' how he didn't know what he was doing until the next day. Shit, I've been waitin' for years for Wayne to grow up and man up. I'm seriously tired of his shit. I want a house, a family, a fuckin' husband I don't have to question every time he opens his mouth." She was fired up like a Iyanla Vanzant moment hit her.

"And having the fool around is gonna bring you closer to that?"

"Having him around to first show him then take it all away will be enough for me to move on. If I'm legit and makin' money why wouldn't I have what I want? I ain't the one doing the porn, nor will I ever be. But—"

"But nothing! Now you know if you give him a title or even the feelin' of him runnin' shit he's gonna take over. Then what? Are you gonna be able to control that?" I interrupted.

"Look"—she scooted to the edge of the sofa—"the way I see it is if I keep him happy for the moment, making it seem like shit is all good, he will want to help. He'll see the money and, besides, you and I both know he won't say no if I suggest that he do a few scenes here and there."

This is what I loved about Cindy; when her mind was set there was no stopping her. *If I played my cards right I might get what I've been curious to know.* I stared at her eyes; there were no more tears, just determination. "Cindy, you know this porn stuff can go left if you let him in on decisions and money for this company. I don't want jump into this shit with you and get slapped in the face with it."

"I know, so . . ." Cindy got up, went into the bedroom, and returned with a blank sheet of paper and a pen. She sat back down, took a magazine off the coffee table, and placed it on her lap with the paper on top of it. Taking the pen in her hand, she wrote the date along with our names.

"What's that?" I asked.

"It's a contract between me and you. This way you can walk at any moment and take your cut. Do you agree?"

I sat up and nodded yes and scratched my head. There were a few things she was forgetting. I didn't want that nigga Wayne to feel he was in control of me. If she wanted this to be business it all had to be clear from the start. "This is all good and I understand why we need this, but you gotta make sure that nigga Wayne plays his part, not that 'you do what I say' bullshit he always doin'."

She stopped writing for the moment. "You let me handle that. Now you gotta play your part as well or this shit ain't gonna work. First, I know I told you to relax on that credit card shit, but we need it, at least twenty-five thousand."

My eyes widened. I held my hand up. "Whoa . . . hold up . . . wait . . . a . . . minute. You want me to get that much on credit cards. How you think that's happenin'? You must want me in jail." I laughed.

Cindy rolled her eyes. "Okay, so tell me how we gonna get the equipment we need? You expect me to use this cash?"

"Why not? You think that shit is easy to get? Cindy, you must not know. I can't just get a credit card with that much money on it without paying for it. Then I could still get popped. Then what?" *Is she serious? What is she thinking?* Thoughts rushed into my mind putting me on the defensive. "So let me get this straight, I'm supposed to get this credit and purchase the equipment with the chance of getting locked the fuck up. You can't be serious,

Cindy. That's a lot of risk I'm taking to start with. You better make that sixty-forty split."

She moved the paper and magazine to the coffee table and sat back on the sofa. "Okay, we gonna work this out. I understand the risk, but do you understand the potential of the money and career you will have? That, I promise you, will be the last time you will have to do something like that. We need that, Sherry. I already found a little house for rent in New Jersey; we can do everything there. The Web shit, the sex tape shit, everything. Once we get some profit and find our little niche we can get a warehouse out there. Make some real money. You see that whole VIP shit you told me about I think we can work a deal with her and use her little sex hustle to carry us to the next level."

"You just think it's that simple, huh?" I shrugged my shoulders and shook my head. "What makes you feel that some next bitch gonna help us? Do you remember where you at? Ain't no bitch givin' anything up if she ain't gettin' a cut of that legit money. Do you actually think bitches is stupid? Besides I don't know her ass from a hole in the wall. How can we trust her? I don't even know her name. Shit, I can't even remember what she looked like!"

"I will take that risk. And I'll pay her out of my percentage. Let me talk to her; I know I can make it happen. Besides I already know ain't no bitch doin' shit for nothin', Miss Sixty-percentage."

We both laughed. I batted my eyes. "Well, I gotta cover my ass if I do get locked the fuck up."

Cindy picked up the magazine and paper again. She quickly wrote another few lines and signed it. Cindy placed it in front me. "Read it and sign it. We will get it notarized tomorrow and open a business account that we both can access."

I looked at the paper and read certain words out loud: "Sixty percent . . . Sexual Desire, LLC . . . All rights incorporated and owned by Cindy Walker and Sherry Pace." I signed it and handed it to her.

"Now, you need to get yo' ass up, go home, take a shower, and see what you can get done today. I will research all the equipment, secure the place, and get somebody I know we can pay daily to shoot the sex scenes and makeup. Like I said I will handle Wayne so don't worry 'bout him. I'm tryin' to have all this shit up and runnin' by the end of the month. That gives us thirty days from now."

"First, I've been up for almost twenty-four hours, so you gonna accept that this nap is well deserved." I closed my eyes and heard her walk out the room mumbling something, but I was too tired to listen or respond. *Will she really come through or will it all fail because of Wayne?* was my last thought before my eyes closed.

Cindy

8

The same day Wayne made his intentions clear, he put fire into me. If he thought I was just going to sit around, cry over him, and wait for him to get his shit together, I had another reaction for his ass. I was completely tired of him. It was time for me to put my big girl panties on and take charge of my life. Following Wayne's actions wasn't benefiting me at all. *He's going to follow my lead or jump ship; either way I will be in control.*

After letting Sherry sleep for most of the day I finally woke her up. I had plans on my mind. She was going to take me back to the strip club. With a fresh mug of coffee in my hand I called her name. "Sherry . . . Sherry . . . Sherry." Finally I saw movement on the sofa.

"Argh . . . What time is it? Damn," Sherry said turning over and partially removing the blanket on top of her.

"It's almost six in the evening. Yo' ass need to get up so we can go the club. I gotta make something happen."

"Who you gonna talk to? Do you think the owners are gonna actually allow you in the club after you left them high and dry? Are you crazy?" She fired off at me as I handed her a cup of coffee. "Thank you."

"It doesn't matter, they ain't gonna know it's me. I'm sure I'm just another girl who couldn't handle it. I want to talk to that VIP chick you bumped into. If I get a one-on-one, I could just make something happen. She's that type of girl where money talks a whole lot louder than the rules I'm sure. I wouldn't start trippin' 'cause that's what you doin'." I rolled my eyes at her and headed toward my bedroom. If she wanted to say anything she was going to get up from the sofa.

I knew exactly what she was doing: delay, delay, and delay some more. I loved her like family, but her drive and motivation fizzled out to quickly for me. *I only hope that I'm making the right decision to get into this business.* The way I saw it, there were two kinds of females: those who actually did what men did and those who liked to pretend they could. Creating a profitable company wasn't only the thing on my mind; it was turning it into a million dollar company to provide for my future.

I started searching through my closet for an outfit. I heard my bedroom door squeak.

"Cindy, what you doin'? Why you wake me up so damn early anyway? The club don't open 'til like nine." Sherry walked toward the closet. "Here put this over there somewhere." She handed me the mug of coffee. "I better dress you for this little encounter."

She pulled dress after dress out of my closet and threw them to the bed. I set the mug on the nightstand and tried to fix the mess she was creating. "Can you stop tossing my clothes on the bed like that? This shit ain't from Target!"

"Girl, please, most of these styles you don't even wear anymore. We might have to go shopping for this. Don't you have some leather shorts somewhere in here?"

"Leather shorts? What about some pants, long-ass pants to cover most of me? I ain't tryin' to go in there half naked." She started to laugh.

"C'mon, Cindy, you're goin' into a strip club to convince a madam to loan you some of her hoes for an IOU. You gotta look like you 'bout to make some money."

I guessed she was right. I couldn't walk in there feeling the part, but not look like I was a money maker. I still hadn't thought of what I was going to say yet, but whatever I did say had to be convincing.

Sherry pulled out mostly everything in my closet onto my bed.

"Okay, you got these red bottoms that you must wear and, let's see, you got these tight black Prada pants." She was picking up hangers with silk shirts; then she placed a blue Christian Dior shirt in front of her.

"Umm, are you now looking for yourself or me?"

"I'm not tryin' to go back to my house so I might as well borrow something from you. You don't mine do you?" She smiled.

I knew whatever she got her hands on I wouldn't get it back. Every time she borrowed anything I never saw it again. I was sure half of her closet had my shit in there. It's all good though; it's only clothes. After picking outfits for herself and me she walked into my bathroom. She didn't bother to close the door. I saw her undress.

I watched her as I pretended to clear off the piles of clothes she left on the bed. Her body captivated me. Flawless brown skin, auburn hair hanging down her back, huge breasts perfectly on her chest; her ass was round and plump with no cottage cheese imprints.

"Cindy . . ."

I jumped at her voice. I was staring at her full frontal naked body. Her nipples were sticking out, big and inviting. Her snatch was neatly waxed.

"Cindy, can you bring me in a towel when you done, please."

I quickly turned around and headed out the room hoping she didn't notice that I was staring at her. This was the first time I felt this way about her or any female. She turned me on. I was pacing back and forth in the kitchen; then I heard the shower running. Did she leave the door open? Was she inviting me? I shook my head and walked into the second bathroom. I pulled back the curtain on the makeshift closet I made Wayne put up for me. I grabbed a towel and a wash rag and headed back to my room. The shower was still running. I announced myself by clearing my throat when I walked in.

"So tell me what you're going to say to her?" Sherry asked.

"Umm, I don't know." My mind wasn't on what I was going to say, but what I was going to attempt with Sherry.

The shower stopped and she pulled the plastic curtain back. I naturally opened the towel out for her. She stepped out of the tub and reached for the towel. Her eyes met mine. She dropped the towel and placed her hand on my face stroking my cheek gently. My lips got closer to hers. Her lips were soft; her body was still wet from the shower. We kissed passionately, my fingers started to pull at her nipples. She started to strip my clothes off. Pushing me against the vanity in the bathroom I lifted myself up onto the sink. She cupped my breast into her hand and sucked on my nipple. I was so horny, my moans grew louder as her tongue played with my nipples. She bowed her head and licked the inside of my thigh. I opened my legs wider, wanting every inch of her tongue to devour me.

"Cindy, are you still there?" She pulled the curtain back suddenly.

Her voice shook me out of my daydream. I handed her the towel and left the bathroom in a hurry. I didn't want her to think I was trying to initiate anything with her. She was my best friend and soon-to-be partner in a very sexual-based enterprise. I had to start this off right and mixing pleasure with business was a bad decision. At this point I didn't need anything that may have put me back five steps.

***

It was half past ten and we were now getting in a cab to head to the strip club. When we arrived I made the cab drop us off down the block from the club. There were a lot of stragglers in front of the club already. I didn't want to be noticed.

"I wonder if there's a back entrance into the club."

"Why we going through the back, Cindy? We hiding from people now?"

"No, but it will be better for us not to be obvious. Keep walking; we'll see what's up." As we walked past the club I saw some Mexicans with aprons on in the alley smoking cigarettes. "C'mon, Sherry, follow me." I walked up to them and lied to gain entrance through the kitchen.

"I didn't know you had it like that." Sherry teased as one of the guys let us in and showed us the way to the girls' dressing room.

There was no one in there, so we quickly exited and went straight toward the VIP area. I told Sherry to look out for the woman she bumped into last time. The music was loud and the dancers were crowding the men at the bar. As we walked by someone squeezed my ass cheek. I didn't stop to turn around and cause a scene; I kept it moving.

We were walking through a very dark hallway, then what seemed like an open space. I was definitely feeling a bit edgy. "Sherry, where the fuck you takin' me?"

"Yeah, ain't this crazy. One female bathroom and it's all the way back here. I don't have to wonder why. They want somebody to get raped back here. Some sick shit."

I looked around and couldn't see much of anything but small red flashing lights up toward the ceiling. "Yo, Sherry, what up with those lights up there?"

"Lights?" Sherry stopped moving and looked up. "What the fuck?" I couldn't see her expression but by the way she jerked on my hand to move quickly, it wasn't good.

"Shit, what the fuck is wrong with you?" I ripped my hand loose from her grip. I noticed my bracelet was gone on my wrist when I touched it. "Shit, I done lost my bracelet 'cause of you!"

"Please, who cares 'bout yo' cheap-ass bracelet? Those little red lights were cameras. So much for us not being noticed."

"Cameras?" *What are they recording?* was the question on my mind.

Soon we were in front of the door Sherry described to me. We peeked in and it was completely dark.

Suddenly a deep voice behind us spoke, "Can I help you ladies?"

My heart skipped a beat with fear causing me to grab a hold of Sherry. "Shit!"

"Can I help you ladies?" He was huge, arms folded across his chest waiting for our answer.

"We were told the bathroom was back here," Sherry said nervously.

"It's right over there. Don't you see the neon sign?" He chuckled a little.

We both turned our heads and walked in quickly.

"Sherry, you didn't mention Big Shawn was gonna be guarding the door! Look I'm just gonna go ask him. This 'bout money. You can stay here if you want to."

I walked out the bathroom and walked up to him. "Can you tell me where I can find the person in charge of this room? My friend in there is a little shy. She was here before and a woman approached her last time 'bout this room. I just want to make sure it's something I want to get into."

"If you can't tell me her name then I can't help you."

I stood there for a minute. "A'ight, I hear you. I guess I'ma have to go bother Frank and Lou. I just hope they don't mind me taking 'em away from taking care of their customers when you can easily help. It seems to be some bigwigs on the main floor. Let me go tell my friend. Thanks." I turned around slowly and moved toward the bathroom door a short distance away.

As soon as my hand pushed the door he said, "Wait, I'm gonna go get her."

I turned around and smiled. "Thank you, sweetheart."

I told Sherry to come out the bathroom. She came out like a scared cat. "Could you not look like that! Smoke a cigarette or something to calm yo' ass down."

"I don't think you can smoke in here," she said with a stink attitude. She was full of shit with all her talk about playing the part and she acting like a scared chicken. Maybe my choice to make her partner was something I had to rethink. I put all that out my mind and noticed a tall, slender woman walking toward me with the same guy behind her.

"Is that her, Sherry?" I whispered.

"Um-hm," Sherry sounded.

The tall, slim woman approached me. "Do I know you? How do you know about the VIP room?"

I looked over to Sherry then back to her. "Do you think you can step away from here for a moment? I have a proposition that would benefit the both of us." I stared at her trying to get a good look at her face.

"You can talk to me here about it."

I move closer to her, inhaling her sweet strawberry smell. I whispered in her ear, "I don't think this would be the right place to talk with all the eyes in the sky. I want you to make some real money not hand over everything to Frank and Lou." I smiled at her.

She tilted her head at me and stepped back. "What you know 'bout Frank and Lou? I ain't never seen you in here, neither yo' friend. Why should I trust y'all?"

Sherry stepped out of her shell and said softly, "You don't remember inviting me to play in the VIP room?"

The slender female took a long stare at Sherry and shook her head. "Yes, yes, I remember you. So, you brought yo' pimp to work out a deal for you?" She laughed loudly.

I didn't find that funny. I wasn't nobody pimp. Sherry was about to get in her face, but I put my hand out to stop her. "I wonder if you maybe scared of money. This is something for you or do you want to work here paying yo' debt off to Frank, Lou, and whoever else they pass you on to."

"You got a lot of balls talkin' 'bout shit you know nothin' of," she said getting in my face.

"I must know something for you to be stink-face like this now. Should we discuss yo' business here or can I invite you out for a drink somewhere so we can discuss this like business women instead of measuring our dicks out in the open?"

"Yeah, a'ight, give me yo' phone."

I reached into my purse and handed her my phone.

She punched in her number and handed it back to me. "Call me in 'bout an hour and we can arrange somethin'."

"What should I call you? I'm assuming you don't like to be called Madam."

Her posture changed to a more open position. "Carmen."

I put my hand out. "I'm Cindy and that's Sherry. I will definitely call you in an hour."

"Yeah, you do that."

Sherry and I walked past her and the huge bouncer back down the dark hallway through the open space. Again we walked past the bar and directly through the front door. It was a big relief that the first step was done—I made contact. Now I had an hour to figure out what I would say.

We had an hour to kill. "Sherry, you want to go into that bar over there?"

"That shit looks like a hole in the wall. Why don't we just go to the diner two blocks from here?"

"A'ight, I'm good with that." I walked beside her concentrating on what I would say to Carmen. I got some insight as to what was going on with her from her responses when we met. I just had to make it sound like she would have a new start. I didn't know what she was into or what exactly she was doing at the strip club.

We walked into the diner and took a booth in the far corner. The diner was pretty empty. I wasn't hungry, but I wanted a drink. When the waitress came to our table I asked for a short glass of vodka and Sherry ordered a coffee. As soon as she returned and placed the glass in front of me I swallowed it all in one shot.

"You better not start that drinking. 'Cause ain't nobody gonna take yo' drunk ass seriously." Sherry sipped on her coffee.

"Nah, it ain't like that. I just needed a little liquid courage." I glanced at my phone clocking the time: 9:45 p.m.

"Yeah, okay." Sherry nodded her head.

We sat there going back and forth with each other about what I should and shouldn't say. If I said I cared about Sherry's input I would be lying. Regardless of what she said I was still going to do and say what I wanted. Sherry may not have liked it, but she didn't have a choice. I was the one taking all the risk. All she done was a big fat nothing!

Sherry was cool, but didn't look her way to go out there and make shit happen. She would rather go with the flow and hope, wish, and pray for something to happen. I was the one who pushed her to get that nurse's aide job. If it wasn't for me her ass would still be collecting welfare and fucking every man she found who would empty their pockets to her. Thank goodness she knew how to be safe—she always used protection because she couldn't afford an abortion nor did she want to be forced to have a miscarriage. At least she was smart about that.

My hands were sweating a little. I wanted another drink. I glanced at my phone: 10:20 p.m. It wasn't an hour yet, but I decided to call her anyway. If she didn't pick up, I would just move on.

"Hey, I was just about to call you," Carmen said.

"I'm over at the diner. You know which one?"

"The one near the club, yeah, I know. I'll see you in ten." The phone clicked.

"Well, I'm glad I called. She's on her way." In the back of my mind I didn't want Sherry there. I didn't want her to fuck this up. I didn't want to be rude either. I knew she would ride or die for me, but this has to be handled on a one-to-one basis. "Sherry, don't take this the wrong way, but I need you to leave. You can go to my crib." I handed her my keys.

"Leave, why?" Her entire posture and demeanor changed. She was pissed. "Tell me why I shouldn't be here if I'm your so-called partner and I'll leave."

"It would just be better. I can't explain it right now."

"You know what, Cindy, fuck you. I don't need to go to yo' house. I got my own. Or did you forget that?"

Her voice was loud; the waitress and the cook came out to see what was happening. I grabbed her hand and squeezed it. "Sherry, you causing a scene. This is not what we need right now. Please go to my house and wait for me. I'll be there once I'm through." I spoke in my calmest and sweetest voice.

"You ain't shit, Cindy." Sherry shook my hand off hers and grabbed her purse out the booth, then walked out without a word.

"Can I get you the check?" the waitress said suddenly.

"No, thanks. I will have some more vodka. Thanks." I felt bad, but it didn't last long. Sherry has to understand this was my business and she was just another name on the contract. It was stupid of me to give her sixty percent of the business, but if this all worked out there would be other businesses where she wouldn't have a percentage— just a paycheck.

After the waitress brought my drink, I saw a tall, slim, fair-skinned woman walking into the diner. Her hair was short and black. She looked in my direction and started walking toward me. *Damn, I didn't think she looked that good,* I thought. Her tight black leather pants showed her huge gap between her legs. It was sexy, especially with the high boots she wore. Her breast was small enough that she didn't need a bra. The silk black tank top fitted loose enough for her erected nipples to stick out. Carmen took a seat in the booth and the smell of strawberries filled my nostrils.

"Hello, Cindy." She put her hand out.

I shook her hand and replied, "Hello, Carmen, I'm happy you came to meet me."

"So, Cindy, tell me why I'm here."

I took a deep breath. "Carmen, I know you don't know me, but I know a way we can help each other out, financially."

"Go on . . ."

"I don't know exactly what you do at the club, but I know you can make more money than what you doing now. I need girls and you have them. I can give you a flat fee for the girls and a percentage on what I make with them."

"Hold on, I ain't no pimp and you ain't about to turn me into one."

"Even if it means making money, legally? I don't know about you, but this under-the-table bullshit is getting old.

Wouldn't you like to secure your future so you can leave that shit behind?"

Carmen's eyes widened. I saw the wheels turning in her mind. Her hands became fidgety. "How much money are we talking about?"

"Well that depends . . ."

"Depends . . . that don't sound secure. If you trying to start an escort service, I'm not interested." She started to move out the booth.

I touched her hand. "Wait, let me explain. I want to start a sex line and Web cam shows online. There's no sex unless the girls want to on camera."

"So you want to start a porn site." She nodded her head.

I hoped by telling her my main objective she wouldn't run and start up her own shit. "Look I don't know what your situation is with Frank and Lou at the club, but I'm sure you know a lot of people to have that VIP room occupied. I just felt that you would want to get out of their grip. Wouldn't you?"

"How do you know Frank and Lou and what they got with me?"

"I don't, but I know you ain't trying to let them in on this opportunity to take more money out yo' mouth."

"I do know some people, but I have to talk to the right person." Carmen tapped on the table twisting her lips.

"Look, how about this: you put me in touch with the right person and I'll do the rest. I will still need a commitment from you that you will provide the girls to do the work. Let's be honest, any one of those girls you got hanging from the ceiling wouldn't mind talking sexually on the phone for the same amount of money, and I definitely don't think we will have any problem convincing them that fucking on camera was any different."

"And what if Frank and Lou find out what I'm doin'? Will you be there to take the bullet or the ass beating I'm going to get?" I laughed. "How would they know what you're doing if I'm the one running the show? I think you have to let me in on what situation you have with them before I put myself in front of that bullet."

"First, ain't nothing funny. Second, Frank and Lou ain't yo' average club owners. I'm sure you knew that already. Third, why did you come to me instead of them?"

I was surprised she remembered me. When I auditioned she was sitting at the bar while I danced. I didn't think she was the one Sherry was talking about. "I'm sorry, I didn't mean to laugh. You're right; I do know they ain't the average, but I can tell you I would love to shut them down. Who's to say that in six months the only girls they'll have dancing look like Big Red?"

Carmen busted out laughing.

"Yeah, you know exactly who I mean, too. Do you know she tried to extort my ass?" I shared.

"She does that to all the newbies. That bitch older than both of us put together. Rumor has it that she's Lou's side chick when Frank stopped him from forcing the girls to fuck him in order to dance that week."

"That's fucked up. So if you had the opportunity to make something yo' own why would you want to still fuck with these bastards? You see I left the first night I danced. I'm telling you it could all work out. I know you know people. From what Sherry saw that night in that room, there's no way you just doing yo' job without communicating with someone who knows someone."

"You're right; the room is used for those who like to add a little spice to their marriage, relationship, or just plain ol' freaks. It's crazy that room is booked six nights a week in two-hour blocks. There's a steady average of fifteen booked sessions per week and then there's the two-way mirror room. Frank came up with the idea of charging a chosen few who attend the club a fee just to look in. They make a killing off that shit."

"So why don't you want to get some of that money legally? I'm sure they ain't doing that shit legally. Every dime is going in their pockets. I bet they ain't putting a quarter of what they make in your pocket. Correct?" I called her on it, hoping she would see what I was offering: freedom.

She bowed her head and continued to tap on the table. I figured the numbers were spinning in her mind and she was determining her worth.

Carmen raised her head. "I gotta make a phone call." She pulled her phone out her back pocket and touched the screen.

There was a phone ringing and I heard a male's voice over the speaker phone. "Hey, what's up?"

"Are you in town?" Carmen asked.

"Yeah, don't tell me you miss me already." He laughed.

"Something like that. I need to talk to you about something that you can help me out with."

"You know I'm always there for you. I told you already if you wanted out I can buy yo—"

Carmen cut him off quickly. "Just meet me at my house later, okay. We can talk then." She ended the call.

"Who was that?" I asked.

"He might be the one to give you some help." She took her phone and typed on the screen.

I felt my phone buzz next to me. I opened my purse and looked at my phone; there was a new text message. *This better not be Sherry,* I thought.

"I just texted you my address. Come by tomorrow after two and you can talk to my guy; then I'll see if I want to fuck with you." She got up from the booth and started to walk out the diner.

I pulled out a fifty dollar bill from my purse and tossed it on the table. I walked out behind her, watching her round ass shift from side to side. She got into a Lincoln Town Car idling at the curb.

She saw me step out the diner and lowered the window. "Do you need a ride back to the club?"

"Nah, I'm headed home. I'll catch a cab."

"No need, hop in. My driver can take you after he drops me off." Carmen opened the door and scooted over.

I got in. "Thanks, you sure it's okay?"

"Why don't you stay with me at the club for a little while?" Carmen asked.

"I don't think that's a good idea for anyone to see me with you. I mean if you serious about making this money I can't be seen in that club with you." I hoped she understood where I was coming from.

"Absolutely right. I'm having a good feeling about this." The Town Car pulled up to the club. "All right, this is me. I'll see you tomorrow."

"Thanks, again."

"Talk soon." She closed the door and walked into the club.

"Where would you like to go?" the driver asked.

I gave him my home address and sat back replaying the entire conversation with Carmen. I realized she never revealed why Frank and Lou would want to kill her if they found out what she was doing. I took my phone out my purse and dialed Sherry. She didn't pick up; it went straight to voice mail. Leaving her a message was useless. Since she was mad at me I probably wouldn't hear from her until she's over it. *Well she better get over it real soon.*

Carmen

9

Soft, gentle kisses were slowly moving up my thigh under the sheets. I know those lips. "Hey when did you come in?" I tugged the sheets off so I could see his beautiful face and eyes. The sunlight was beaming through the windows of my room so it had to be early morning.

"Does it matter?" He slowly pulled my panties off and opened my legs wide. His wet tongue teased my bare pussy.

"Ahh . . ." He stuck his tongue deep into my flesh. It made my body want him even more. I twisted my hard nipples. "Suck it hard, baby. Yeah, that's it." I grabbed at his hair and pushed his head deeper between my legs. I was about to climax. "I'm cumming . . ." I released my grip and he lifted his head. When I came I squirted directly into his open mouth. He loved it when I squirted all over his face.

"Yeah, give me that," he said between swallows. He pushed my legs behind my head and licked every inch of my sweetness before inserting his cock into me. He liked it rough so he smacked me around as he rammed into me. "Yeah, bitch, you like this big white dick don't you?"

"Yes, baby, fuck yo' pussy. Make me hurt, baby." I held my legs behind my head allowing all of him to slam into my hot box. His roughness was tolerable and soothing to my sexual appetite. He allowed others to join and sometimes he even permitted my fantasy to play out.

"I want you to squirt all over me. Are you cumming?"

"Pull on my nipples and fuck me harder . . ."

He pumped into me faster and deeper while pinching my nipples. It was getting me hotter.

"That's what you want, bitch?" He smacked me across my face.

"Do it again." He did as I asked.

My clit was pulsating; it was ready to explode. "I'm gonna cum, baby . . . I'm cumming . . . Ahhh . . ." I squirted all over him as he continued to fuck my pussy.

"Yeah, baby, I love that shit. Rub on your clit."

I did as he said and I squirted some more on him. He was moving slowly in and out of me. I could feel all the wet, sticky cum all over his chest as he lay on top of me. I let go of my legs and wrapped them around his waist.

After a few strokes he eased out of me and tapped me on my stomach. "C'mon, baby, you know what I really like. Let me fuck you like I used to."

I smiled and flipped over exposing my round ass. I perched it up in the air. He entered me slowly. It felt so normal for him to fuck me in my ass. I never wanted him to stop. When he climaxed so did I. He dropped on the bed next to me.

"Remember how we didn't think this could happen."

"We found a way didn't we? I told you I would take care of you, even when you tried to leave. I told you all ready you are the only one who knows me, all of me. All those other chicks didn't matter. You know that right?"

"I know I'm not worried about you leaving me. Besides you can't because you know yo' ass don't want yo' secret out." I laughed and so did he.

"You said you had something to talk to me about. Have you finally decided about Frank and Lou?"

"Yes and no."

He sat up in bed. "What's that supposed to mean?"

"Okay, before you say no listen to what I have to say. Okay, promise me." I waited for his words.

"Why does this sound like I'm about to be conned?"

"Really, was it a con when I lied to the Feds about yo' whereabouts and shit? Stop playing with me. Just make the promise so I can tell you." I was pissed that he would even say that word. I jerked at the sheets to show my attitude.

"All right, stop. I didn't mean to make you upset. I promise, now how can I help?"

"I met this chick and she wants to get into some porn shit, but legally. Not like Frank and Lou either, where they're the ones pocketing all the money. You and I both know they don't throw me no more money than they should; the rest gets chalked up to the debt I owe. She proposed that I provide the girls, and I get a set fee and a percentage of whatever profit she makes off of them. Since you got the connections with the Armenians and Polish why can't we use those girls and turn double the profits without them knowing? I'm sure if we give the girls some money on the side we could keep their mouths shut when they get shipped around. And I could use some of the girls from the club easy. They so damn desperate they'd be happy to fuck for a guaranteed fee."

"Sounds like you already worked out a deal."

"No, this chick don't know what she's doing and that's where you come in. I want you to come in and show her what to do; you know, use that same charm that gets you into most politicians' pockets. Put the deals in front of her, get everything in her name, push her to your lawyers for contracts and accountants for the profits. Can't you have them word those contracts in a way that you will own the rights and a percentage of the royalties?"

"Aren't you worried about her reading those contracts?"

"She ain't if you play your role correctly; and besides she's hungry and don't know nothing. I mean if she knew me she would have ran in the opposite direction. Listen, she's a nobody who could probably get us back to where we want to be. I just need your connections to get her started and maybe a little incentive. I know she hasn't even thought about getting a place, office space, packaging . . . you know all that stuff."

"Have you talked to her about that or do you need me to set it all up?" He was a bit hesitant.

"Hell no, I want her to feel like she's in control. Besides, I think we can make double than when you was fucking with them foreigners."

"How is that?" He was intrigued now.

I knew after the Feds tried to charge him with trafficking he stopped fucking with the sex trade for a moment, but once all of the indictments were cleared he got back into it. He had a great thing going: they supplied the girls and he put them out there to earn with the pretense of getting citizenship. It was easy to keep the girls happy and after a while they wouldn't even question the citizenship promise. If any one of the girls started to act up he would ship them off elsewhere to get turned out into something worse than what they'd become.

"I think this can give you an opportunity to make more money because it's a legit business in someone else's name. Do you think the Feds are still watching you?"

"Carmen, they don't ever stop. The way I move they have to jump through crazy hoops and barriers just to talk to me again, all thanks to my lawyer. Besides you know I never stay in the same place for more than a week or two. But if this is legit then we may be able to wash a few mil for a few friends, and that, my dear, sweet Carmen, will put us where we won't need to do shit but sit back and collect. Then just maybe we can settle down somewhere on the other side of the world of course." He jumped off the bed showing his excitement.

"Okay, you need to meet Cindy and get her started. What time is it anyway?" I scanned around the room for my phone.

"It's almost ten. Why?" He looked at me funny then took a seat at the edge of the bed.

"Cindy should be over here sometime after two. I told her to come through. I would rather you not be here."

"Why not?"

"I don't want her to feel . . . I don't think we should let her know how close we really are. Keep it business-like, you know that way everything will be smooth. Just promise me you won't bring her into my bed!" I tapped him lightly on the arm with my fist.

"Ahhh, okay I won't bring her into your bed . . ." He had a devilish grin on his face. I knew what that meant—he may not bring her into my bed but nothing would stop him from fucking her everywhere else.

I had accepted that after all these years he would never be my one and only. It didn't matter anymore because he always took care of me regardless of how much trouble I got into or how far I strayed away. He accepted me for who I was, not what everyone else wanted me to be.

"All right, I better head out of here then. Why don't you bring her to Houston's in the city and we can have a late lunch. One request, make sure I'm not wasting my time."

I pulled him toward me and gave him a kiss on the lips. "I promise you're going to love how easy this will be."

"Yeah, we'll see. Let me get dress and get my ass out of here. But you still haven't said anything about Frank and Lou." He kissed me on my cheek and got dressed. He was waiting for my answer.

"I still haven't decided. It's very touchy and it's family."

"Okay, but you can't go on this way without telling them the truth. It's been two months and they still asking me about that night." He was right but I wasn't ready to face that truth.

I was only thinking of how set we would be once Cindy got started. I wouldn't have to come clean about anything. I could leave New York for good.

The surprising knock at my door made me jump. Usually the main entrance door into the building was locked. I glanced at my watch. It was almost two so this had to be Cindy. *Damn, ain't she punctual.* I walked over to the door. "Who is it?" I looked through the peephole.

"Cindy," she said in a low voice.

I opened the door, "Hey, come on in. Have a seat." I saw her eyes getting bigger as she walked in.

"Damn, girl, I didn't think Harlem had shit like this. Can I get a tour?" Cindy blurted out.

I didn't expect her to show her brownnosing skills that early. "Yeah, but it ain't much. It's a one-bedroom duplex. Well, I'm lying; it's really a two-bedroom, but I had the second bedroom turned into my closet. It cost me an arm and a leg, but it's my little piece of heaven on earth. The bedroom is upstairs. I would take you but it's a mess."

"This is nice." She was staring at the custom-designed kitchen: long marble-top center island, huge glass refrigerator doors, wide six-burner stove with double ovens beside it. The stools along one side of the center island were wide bottomed with leather fabric covering them.

"Thanks; why don't you have a seat so we can get down to business. Do you want something to drink?" I pointed her to the white leather sectional in the living room.

"Hmm, do you have some bottled water? If not I'm cool."

Bottled water? Not a glass, but a bottle! Was she serious? Did she think I was gonna get her drunk or some shit? I turned my back and opened the fridge to get her a bottle of water. My attitude was turned up a little.

"Thanks," she said grabbing the bottle out my hand. "You have a really nice place."

"Thanks, but you should really strive for more. This is just a little something that I hope to sell real soon. Hey, maybe if we make a lot of money with the porn thing you trying to do you can buy it from me. Trust me I'll give you a fair price."

She giggled. "Well, why don't you tell me how you can help me make this happen?"

"Yes, well there's someone I want you to meet. But before you do meet him I want you to know what you want. This guy is no joke. He can make it all happen for you, but you have to listen to his advice."

"Wait, hold on, Carmen, it sounds like you already made my decision for me. I don't want you to feel that I don't appreciate this, but let's be honest; just like you don't know me I don't know this dude. And business is run strictly on money and ambition. Ambition I have lots of, money I don't. Basically can this guy fund my start-up and set me up with the right people? Not that crazy shit Frank and Lou got at the club either, 'cause I know that shit ain't no way close to legal. I want my shit to be legal and on the up-and-up. I was hoping you would provide the girls for the sex lines and the Web shows; then maybe later on we can move into making the porn and selling it."

"Oh, he can make all that happen and more. The question here is, are you willing to do what it takes to make it happen for yo'self? I mean you can lead a horse to water, but you can't make him drink it. Listen, there's no problem in getting the girls to fill the positions. There's a whole lot of dreamers out there who love to live in the fantasy."

"Well, that's all fine but if I don't feel your friend then it's a bust, unless you put up the capital and we do this to help each other. Now, you never answered my question about Frank and Lou back at the club. What's your situation there? What exactly will I be taking a bullet for?"

Of course I didn't want to put my shit out there so I tiptoed around it. "First, it ain't that serious. It's some shit that happened way back when and now I just have to work off a debt I owe."

"Well, it can't be that bad with a place like this. Okay, so when do we meet your friend?"

"I thought we could go now. What happened to yo' friend by the way? What was her name again?"

"Sherry. She is my partner so I want her to be there with me. Tell me where so I can text her where to meet us."

I had a confused look on my face. "Why don't you meet with him first, let him lay out whatever he can offer, and then bring her in? I mean you don't want to look stupid if this shit ain't what you want." I needed her to be sold on the bigger picture first before involving little birdies chirping in her ear.

She stared at me with her phone in her hand. By her silence I knew she was replaying my words and tone in her mind.

"I guess you're right. When we leaving?"

"Let me go get my purse and shoes upstairs; then we could leave."

"Sounds good."

I got up from the sectional and walked to the iron circular staircase leading upstairs. *So far, so good.* I didn't worry about the meeting. Everything was going to work out just fine. Cindy was going to do what she needed to do and I was going to turn that into my gold mine.

Sherry

10

This bitch Cindy got some nerve. After two days of not talking to me she didn't even pick up the fucking phone. She sent me a text instead, demanding that I come to her house ASAP. She didn't even have the courtesy to talk to me after she kicked me out at the diner and pushed me to the side. I didn't know what she was doing, if we were still doing this together or if she was flying solo. Cindy probably thought I was going to call her to beg for her forgiveness. I refused to bow down to her stupid holier-than-thou attitude. She had to reach out to me first after that bullshit she did at the diner.

I wasn't going to not show up, but I sure as hell was going to make her ass wait until I was good and ready. I purposely waited twenty minutes before I texted her back. Did she think I was going to jump because she finally wanted to talk to me? *Please that bitch better make sure she tells me everything before I leave her ass to fall on her face.* I may not have wanted to wipe old people's asses but it paid my bills. Besides my credit card scams were almost perfect.

It was nice outside so I decided to walk instead of calling a cab. It only took me about fifteen minutes to walk to her house. As I walked along Eastern Parkway my phone kept buzzing with her name and number flashing across the screen. I refused to press answer at first but after the fifth call and seventh text I'd had enough.

"Cindy, what the fuck yo'? I'm on my fuckin' way." My voice was loud.

"Damn, you can leave that shit at the door when you get here."

"Wait, hold up, you don't fuckin' call me after you met up with Carmen. Then you text me like shit all good. Bitch, I ain't talk to yo' ass for two days. What the fuck is all that about? Come downstairs and open the fuckin' door." I pressed end on my phone screen. Cindy was about to see me in a different light because when you're forming a business together with someone, you don't shut them out.

About a minute later the front door opened. Cindy had her hand on her hip with a stink face. "Why you actin' like that? You ain't even give me a chance to give you the lowdown. Did you think for one second that maybe I was trying to put everything in place before I brought yo' ass into it!"

"Is that what you call it?" I stood there, lightly laughing.

"You're crazy. So what you trying to say?" I couldn't believe her question, as if there was nothing to be mad about.

"Cindy, you can't be serious right now! Your ass told me we was startin' a business together, bitch, but yet you ain't talk to me since you pushed me to the side. I'm not about to go all out if you keeping shit to yo'self. Why am I here then? Go do that shit with yo' so-called ex all by yo'self."

Cindy's face turned red as if I caught her hand in the cookie jar.

"So tell me, what the fuck am I doin' here? Was me signing papers and shit a game? Are you frontin' now? Let me guess, you partnering up with Carmen now, right?" I folded my arms across my chest and waited for her response.

"No, stupid, but I sure as hell ain't getting into it with you at my front door. Can you come inside?" She turned around and headed inside.

Cindy pissed me off, but I wasn't mad enough to walk away from a definite come up. I swallowed my pride and attitude and followed her in. I shut the door behind me then walked into her living space and took a seat on the armchair. "So talk."

"Well, damn—"

"Well, damn, nothing. You the one actin' brand new. I can't read minds and you ain't talked to me for two days so how the fuck am I supposed to know what's goin' on?" I cut her off immediately; if anyone was going to have an attitude it was going to be me only.

Cindy stared at me seated on the sofa. She suddenly stood up and headed into her kitchen. I watched her intently; she opened a cabinet and pulled out two glasses, then opened another cabinet door and pulled out a bottle of Yellowtail red wine. Standing in the kitchen she opened the wine and filled both glasses and headed back into the living space.

"Here let's have a drink," Cindy said with a smile on her face and handed me a glass.

"I'm not thirsty," I said standoffish.

"Okay." Cindy put the glass on the coffee table in front of me and continued, "Look, Sherry, I'm not feeling the fucking stink-ass attitude you got. The reason I kicked yo' ass out of the diner was only 'cause I didn't want you to fuck it up in any way. You know sometimes you talk just a little too much and that shit rubs people the wrong fuckin' way. Don't act like I ain't right either." She took a seat on the sofa and sipped at her glass of wine.

I was holding myself back from slapping the shit out of her. "First of all why don't *you* stop actin' like such a great friend if you really got other intentions? Cindy, why did you even ask me to quit my job and help you if yo' ass was just gonna push me to the side like a Facebook buddy? What the fuck I'm supposed to think? I ain't stupid. Are you tryin' to cut me out since you met Carmen?" *She better answer me correctly because if she don't it's going to get real in here with the quickness.* I decided to grab the glass of wine off the table and sip on it. If she only knew what I was thinking: *This bitch don't know I'm ready to shove this glass down her motherfuckin' throat.*

"Stop that shit, okay, Sherry? It ain't even like that. I wanted to make sure everything was legit and not give us the runaround. What if you was there and she said some bullshit? You woulda bashed Carmen's head in for wasting our time. Tell me that ain't true and I'll give you an eighty-five–fifteen split on all the money we 'bout to make." She smiled putting her glass in the air.

I couldn't help but to smirk at her. "Whateva, go get that bottle then tell me how well you set everything up." I tapped her glass gently with mine. I didn't know what to expect, but I was willing to listen especially when it has to do with money.

Cindy walked her happy ass over to the kitchen to snatch the wine bottle off the countertop, and returned to the sofa. She swooped in right next to me and poured more wine into my glass.

"Okay, so my conversation with Carmen went real smooth; she opened my eyes to a few things. This could be bigger than we even imagined. When we meet this dude—"

"Meet this dude? You mean, you ain't even talk to this dude yet!" I almost spilled the glass of wine over all myself. She hadn't called me in days and she talking about meeting some dude. This bitch was seriously smoking some new shit.

"Calm down, Sherry, damn. I met him already and got the scoop. He's supposed to drop by in about an hour and drop off some cash. Girl, we are going to be rich. First, don't trip when you see him. He's not the average dude we hang out with." She sipped some more wine.

"What the hell does that mean? He ain't average. What nigga we fuck with who's average? Girl, you better lay it all out before this 'dude' gets here." I was on edge and unsure of the kind of mess Cindy got into. Did she know where this dude was from? Who he fucked with? How deep his pockets were? I put the glass down on the coffee table.

"First he's a white boy, a fine one, too. Tall, built like a model off *GQ* magazine, blond hair, ocean blue eyes, sexy tats all over his arm and neck. You know how I love a man with tats."

I pulled my head back confused on how excited she was when she described him. I couldn't believe she was already feeling him in that way. "Why do you sound so fuckin' excited about this dude? Who the fuck is he? What the fuck can he do for us? Why is he dropping money off to you?" I had to hit her like a steamroller with questions.

Cindy's eyes widened.

"I mean you don't know this dude. Better question is, do you trust this dude? Do you trust Carmen?"

"Sherry, why wouldn't I? I have to in order to build relationships. You should know that. Listen, just listen. Stop with all the negative questions and shit. Just fuckin' listen to me. This shit is going to take the fuck off. You act like I can't read a person. I read yo' ass."

"What's that supposed to mean?" I twisted up my lips.

"Bitch, you slicker than Swiper the fox. Don't take offense, but you got more street smarts than anyone I know including stupid-ass Wayne. That's why you meeting him now. He said if we start off with Web cam shows that would boost us into the next level—recording the shows and selling them online. He said there's a much bigger world out there than sex lines. I bet in six months you will have that apartment you wanted in Park Slope and I could finally move to the city. Shit, I could see the shopping sprees now."

The doorbell buzzed.

"This must be him." Cindy got up quickly and rushed to the door. She took a look in the mirror on the wall before opening the door.

"Hello," he greeted Cindy, then handed over a neatly wrapped bottle of liquor with a red bow tied around it.

"You didn't have to bring anything. Come in, come in, thank you so much."

I didn't bother to get up from the sofa, but I could see an outline of him. He was tall and definitely out of a *GQ* magazine. Cindy was right, he was fine—if I never wanted to fuck a white boy, he would change my mind in less than a second. I flashed a fake smile.

"You must be Sherry." He walked over and reached out his hand to mine. "Heard a lot about you. I'm confident you will be the perfect woman for the job." He took a seat on the sofa across from me.

I scanned his tats to make sure none were gang affiliated. Cindy didn't know anything about that. "And you are?"

He turned to Cindy for a second then back to me and smiled. "I'm sorry. My name is Daniel McConnelly. I'm going to help you make millions."

"Millions, huh? How you gonna do that?" I was skeptical.

"I was hoping Cindy filled you in." He looked to Cindy again.

"Umm, Daniel, I don't want to be pushy, but I don't see any other bags in yo' hands. Didn't we discuss start-up monies?" Cindy responded.

"Of course, give me your account number and routing number so I can wire you the money right now. What did we say, fifty grand?"

"Fifty bands? How we suppose to pay you back? If you're a loan shark Cindy made a mistake and we don't want nothing you offering."

"Sherry." Cindy threw me a look. "We can discuss this later. He's not a loan shark."

Daniel stood up and walked toward the door.

"Where are you going?" Cindy asked.

"It's obvious your partner has not agreed to what we discussed. I'm not about to sit here to convince you; if you want to do this shit legally you need to do it correctly. That means getting a place, getting a crew, holding auditions for videos, and meetings with top sex industry executives to distribute your videos across the states. Do you guys not want that? Are you guys missing the bigger picture with this silly high school bickering?" He chastised us like kids.

I felt like shit after those questions. Cindy was right; I did talk too much.

"Daniel, please sit down. It's my fault Sherry's not up to speed," Cindy chimed in.

"Look, I gotta make a phone call real quick. I'm going to step outside for a few. When I come back I hope we can make this happen," he said to Cindy as he walked out the door.

"Sherry, what the fuck are you doin'? You about to fuck up this fifty we 'bout to get to jumpstart this off. What the fuck is yo' problem?" She was waving her finger in my face.

"Cindy, get yo' fuckin' finger out my face before I start waving my fist in yo' face. Tell me the fuckin' deal and stop bullshitting around. Trust me, if we can't agree, he's right, this ain't gonna work."

"He's putting up the start-up money; we pay him back when we get our distribution deal. All he wants is a small percentage of the whole, which I think ain't bad if he's giving us all his connections. He even gave me numbers of lawyers, accountants . . . Girl, this shit is the real deal. We gotta take this; if we don't we gonna be selling our asses out there!"

"Oh, hell I ain't selling my ass! And exactly what am I doing in all of this?" I plainly asked my position.

"What you mean? You gonna be running the shit while I run around to all those meetings we gonna have 'cause of Daniel."

"And what 'bout Wayne? Ain't he a part of this shit too?"

"You don't worry 'bout asshole Wayne. I'll take care of him. So, you in or what? He gonna walk in here any minute now."

Daniel knocked on the door and entered. "So, ladies, what's the verdict? Am I walking out of here with confidence to proceed to set up deals for you guys or what?"

"Yes, you are. Let me go get you that account info." Cindy closed the door behind him and walked into the bedroom.

"I'm glad you worked out your differences," Daniel said.

"Yeah, me too. So tell me how long have you been in this business?" I walked over to the sofa and had a seat.

"I do some distribution deals on the side and I have a few adult Web sites. I know a lot of people so I can really help you get this off the ground. Put it this way, I make sure you make money. Now, you guys have to do the work. I'll talk to Cindy more once she sees the lawyer and accountants."

"How do you know Carmen?" Now I was just being nosey.

"Well, I guide her on how to make that VIP room steady income. All those who participate have options. They can get there sexual experience on video for memory or get paid a one-time fee for performing. Their faces aren't shown anyway; they wear masks."

"Okay, here you go." Cindy handed him a Post-it note with writing on it.

I heard the door open.

"Wha . . . Who the fuck is this motherfucker?"

Ahh, shit this was going to blow up in Cindy's face. I got up from the couch hoping Wayne's mind wouldn't create a different picture. Hopefully he wouldn't show out or, even worse, start beating Daniel's white ass. I pulled my phone out and held it in my hand just in case this got out of hand.

"Hold up, Wayne, don't come in here like you run shit. You don't live here no more, remember? Matter of fact give me my key back."

"You still ain't answer me. Who the fuck is this?" He pointed to Daniel.

"His name is Daniel McConnelly. He's helping us with moving forward on our business venture. What are you even doing here?"

Daniel looked to Wayne then Cindy as they threw words back and forth. He didn't look uncomfortable or scared. He tucked the Post-it note into his pocket and walked directly out the door. I guess he understood it was a personal argument that had nothing to do with him.

"Since when you fuckin' with white boys? Sherry, I think you should leave," he shouted at me and Cindy.

"Nigga, please if you think I'm leaving here with yo' ass on the verge of who knows what you got another thing comin'!" I looked over to Cindy. "Should I call the police?" I had my phone in my hand ready to push send.

"Get ready 'cause he got two minutes to get the fuck out my house after that bullshit." She walked past Wayne and closer to the open door. "Wayne, if you can't sit down and talk about who that guy was then you need to leave right now. 'Cause I'm not doing this with you any longer. You and I are through with no hope of ever getting back together. If you want a relationship it will be business only. I advise you to take the opportunity 'cause there's some big money to be made."

I was surprised that she actually gave him an ultimatum. I was used to her giving into his rants and raves. This time she held her own and maybe he finally got the hint that pushing her around wasn't going down anymore. The look on his face was priceless: confused and bewildered. He realized he lost his control.

"Wayne, are you listening to me?" Cindy wasn't playing with him anymore. "Wayne, are you ready to talk about this shit or do I need to call the cops to get you out of here?"

He looked to me then her, then back to me again like he was waiting for my ass to speak.

"So you'll get me locked up if I don't leave, but you're inviting me to stay and hear you talk about some fuckin' white guy who was in my fuckin' house! What the fuck I'm supposed to do?" His voice was loud.

"Wayne, this is not yo' place anymore. You don't share this space with me anymore. We are not together anymore. Now, either you gonna leave *my* fuckin' house or you have a seat and listen to my ass for once." She closed the front door forcing his choice. Secretly I knew she wanted the best for him and sure as hell didn't want his ass locked up.

"What is some white dude gonna do for me that I can't do for myself?"

"First, who the fuck cares if he white! Sit down, fool; you want something to drink?"

"No." He didn't take a seat.

"Fine. I'm getting into the porn business."

Wayne's face immediately turned to me. "What kind of shit you got m . . . Cindy tied into? Do you know who this guy is? Who he deals with? Did you find out any of that shit before pulling the trigger on something you have no clue about?"

"'Cause you always into some illegal shit that will get not only yo' ass locked but my ass too. It's time you stop all that bullshit and maybe build a career in what you love most: fucking bitches."

"Yo, Sherry, can you leave so we can have a private conversation, please," he said calmly.

"I'm not leaving." I stood firm.

"There's no reason for her to leave, Wayne. Listen, either you want in on this and you help out or you walk out that door and don't look back. You make the decision 'cause I'm jumping into the fire with no second thoughts. He's putting up the start-up cost and schooling me on how to make it happen in this business. I'm not going to ask you again 'cause I ain't begging you."

"Yeah, whateva," he said turning toward the door.

"Let him go 'cause we don't need his ego fuckin' up our shit. So let his ass go," I added.

He opened the door and stood there for a moment. Wayne reached into his pocket and pulled out a key chain. "Here is yo' key. Make sure my shit is packed and ready to be picked up in the morning."

"So that's it. You're just leaving without answering me."

"I'm not answering you 'bout nothing until I find out who this dude is. You should be smart and do the same before rushing into something you have no clue 'bout."

"You know what, Wayne, maybe you shouldn't be involved in my shit." She moved toward the door and opened it. She snatched the key chain out his hand and gestured for him to leave.

Closing the door behind him, she looked to me with tears in her eyes. *Here we go; she's going to go back on her word. I knew she wouldn't stick to it. She will never be able to truly let him go.*

"Fuck him, Cindy, why you need his ass anyway? Let him be." I grabbed her hand and led her back to the sofa and filled her glass with some more wine.

"I can't believe his ass. Maybe it would be better just to leave his ass alone."

"Yo, Cindy, check yo' account let's see if Daniel did what he said."

"Do you actually think after what he saw he's still going to fuck with us?" She went into her room and brought out her laptop. After firing it up and tapping on the keyboard she saw her account. She was silent with her mouth wide open. "Sherry, look." She turned her laptop to me.

$55,098.87 Total Balance showed on the screen. "Cindy, this shit is for real. He wasn't lying. Give his ass a call." She still didn't move. "Cindy, call him," I shouted at her.

Cindy finally moved and went into her room for her cell phone. Her hands were shaking as she tapped the screen. She put the phone on speaker.

"Hello," Daniel answered.

"Hey . . . umm . . . umm." She was nervous for some reason.

"Hey, Daniel, its Sherry. We got the money; now, besides getting a place and a crew, what else do we need do?"

"Well, you have to get a crew. I'll text Cindy a few names of some people who can help. Ladies, you have two weeks to get this all set up. I've already sent your first contract over to the lawyer; he's expecting you in his office by morning to sign."

"Is this for real, Daniel?" Cindy finally spoke.

"Cindy, I'm not here to play games. I make money and this is a money maker. Now if you want to back out that's fine, take the money as a loan, but I can't consult you without a fee."

"And what's yo' fee?" I asked.

"You won't be able to afford it. So is that what you want?"

"No, we are with you. Text me the lawyer's number and I will make arrangements with him. Sherry will handle getting a crew together. I will talk you again in the week." Cindy pressed end on the phone screen. She let out a big scream: "Yeahhhhh!"

"I guess we got some work to do." I slapped her high five and we both jumped around like little schoolgirls who just got asked to the big dance.

When I saw all that money it was a good sign. We were about to do some big things. After jumping around like fools we got to work coming up with a plan. First a place, then the crew; immediately we jumped on the Web researching places out in Jersey. We decided a warehouse would be the best; that way we would dress it up how we needed it to look with enough space to have different scenes.

It all came together. We stayed in making calls; Cindy talked mostly to Daniel while I did all the work. I felt a way at first, but realized this would bring stability and real money that I didn't have to scam for. This was good, but in the back of my mind it just felt too good to be true.

Wayne

11

I walked out of Cindy's place with a bad taste in my mouth. I couldn't believe she started fucking with white boys. Who the fuck was he? Why was Sherry there? I headed over to Dee's place to clear my head and decipher what the fuck Cindy was really getting into.

I spotted a gypsy cab and hopped in. Dee lived in Flatbush, at least twenty minutes from Cindy. I sat in the cab repeating what Cindy said, how he was going to make shit happen. I didn't even know how this dude Daniel even got into the circle. I had to talk to Sherry even if I didn't want to. If his ass was in the sex business there had to be someone I knew who heard of him. Shit, he wasn't the only one who knew people.

The cab came to a stop. I pulled out a twenty dollar bill and tossed it to the driver, then headed into Dee's building. After walking up two flights and down a piss-smelling hallway I reached her door and knocked the door.

"Hey, baby, I didn't know you were coming here today. I thought you said you were handling some business shit." She opened her arms.

"What does it matter? I'm here for good now." I walked in without hugging or kissing her like she expected.

"Why you sound like that?" she questioned.

"Sound like what?"

"Sound like you fuckin' just came from a funeral."

"Bitch, please don't start yo' shit now. If you do I'll go stay at a hotel until I find a place," I told her.

Her eyes became watery.

"C'mon, I don't need yo' cryin' shit either. Ain't this what you wanted? Didn't you want me to leave Cindy? Well, I did." I twisted everything around to make sure she felt that I did it for her. I wasn't going to tell her my plans; besides she wasn't in my future.

She took a deep breath and wiped her eyes. "I'm sorry, daddy, what can I do for you?"

I couldn't help myself. "Get on yo' knees." Since she asked it was the least I could do but oblige her offer.

"Mmmm, why don't we take it to the bedroom . . . " She pulled on my hand leading me to her room.

I stood there as she unbuckled my belt and pulled my pants down. My dick was already semi-hard. When she took me into her mouth my dick instantly became hard by her warmth. She moved slowly, making my dick reappear and disappear into her wet mouth.

"Faster, I want to cum," I demanded.

She jerked and sucked me faster as I commanded. My climax was quick and messy. I shot my load all over her face.

"Go get me a rag," I said.

She returned with cum still stuck to her face and handed me the rag. I wiped my dick off and pulled up my pants then tossed her back the rag. "Get that shit off yo' face."

Dee took the rag and wiped her face off. It was disgusting. I wished she wouldn't have done that in front of me. At that moment I decided I couldn't stay there. I buckled my belt and headed to the door.

"Daddy, where you goin'?"

"I'll be back," I lied walking out the door.

I didn't know where I was going, but I sure as hell didn't want to be with her. I pulled out my phone and called Sherry.

"Yo, I need to talk to you. When can you meet me?" I got straight to the point.

"Wayne?"

Why she playing stupid? "Sherry, stop actin' stupid and just tell me when we could meet."

"Well, I'm kinda busy at the moment and I got a lot of shit planned for the upcoming week." It was like she was saying that shit just to rub it in.

"Look I don't want to fuck up anything that will bring you money, but I don't trust this dude and I need to know more 'bout him. I love Cindy and want to make sure this dude ain't taking advantage of her."

"A'ight, I'll call you once I can get some info from Cindy 'cause I'm in the dark just like you."

"Yeah, that sounds doable. We'll talk soon."

"Yeah." The phone clicked.

I looked at my phone and scrolled through my contacts. I had a really good friend out in Chi town that I hadn't spoken to in a while. I dialed her up.

"Who's this?" a raspy voice answered.

"Yo, it's me Wayne," I answered, hoping it was the person I needed.

"Wayne, from NY?"

"Yeah, bitch, what other Wayne you know from NY?"

"Yo, my nigga! I ain't heard from yo' ass since my sister got into that little bullshit. What's up?"

"You still fuckin' with the ladies?"

"Oh, hell yeah, it's a bigger game now."

"Bigger game? What you mean by that?" *What could be bigger than selling pussy?* I questioned myself.

"Look, I can't get into it on the phone, but if yo' ass come through I could show you what's the deal. Give you a tour and shit," she joked around.

"A'ight, tell me one thing: have you heard of some dude named Daniel McConnelly?"

"Daniel McConnelly . . . umm, how he look?"

"White." I laughed a bit.

"He in my business or the other side of things?"

"Umm, that's the problem. I'm not sure. Yo, Carla, this some serious shit. I need to know somethin' 'bout this dude. It's 'bout money."

"Yeah, a'ight, nigga. I'ma call you. But you should come out here. One." The phone went dead.

If Carla didn't know this fool then Daniel was a con artist taking advantage of my Cindy and that was something I wouldn't allow, regardless of how she felt about me. I had nothing with me but the clothes on my back. My pockets were filled though. I wasn't going to Cindy's and I damn sure wasn't going back to Dee's. My options were slim to none. I decided to go meet Sherry first then make a decision 'bout Chi town. Either way, if I wanted to know more about Daniel I had to get over there to talk to Carla face to face.

I was pacing back and forth in front of the Brooklyn LIU campus when Sherry walked up on me.

"I'm here," Sherry spoke.

"Oh, shit, you scared the crap out of me. Don't walk up on people like that. You from the street; you should know better."

She started to turn around to walk away.

"Yo, Sherry, stop. Thanks for coming to see me. Now tell me about this Daniel 'cause I just don't trust this whole shit. It's too good to be true. Why is this dude giving up money to chicks he don't even know? How did Cindy meet him?"

"I brought Cindy back to that club she danced at and we met Carmen, who introduced Cindy to Daniel. He told her that he could make her business into a multimillion dollar company. I met him that same day you showed up at Cindy's. Matter of fact he wired her fifty bands to get everything started."

"Fifty bands? Just like that? Without y'all having shit, but a few ads for sex lines. Don't you think that's too easy?"

"Yeah, at first, but he's already got us a hundred-thousand dollar contract with a distribution company called Vivid Entertainment. So far I don't see any scam and you know I can spot those a mile away," she said with confidence.

"Yeah, you supposed to. But that's all you know 'bout him? Have you even talked to him?" Her answers weren't sitting good with me. It was clear that I had to find out exactly who and where this motherfucker came from.

"A'ight, if you through with the interrogation I gotta go. I just wish you would just be happy for us and see what Cindy's tryin' to offer you instead of hatin'." She rolled her eyes back.

"Look, Sherry, if this shit is on the up-and-up I'ma be the happiest one for y'all. Shit, and if I can get in where I fit in I'm straight. Facts."

"A'ight, Wayne, just don't fuck our shit up, that's all I'm saying. I gotta go." Sherry waved a good-bye and left me there.

Fifty bands, was the only thought in my head. Who the fuck was this man to throw that kind of money to some nobodies? I wasn't putting Cindy down, but I had to look at this from all angles. *Why would he even want to fuck with these bitches? What do they have that he wants?* And if he fucked with Carmen, there had to be something he was after.

With all those questions entering my mind I headed to the club where Carmen worked. I figured on talking to the bartenders and dancers so I could get the scoop on Carmen.

Carmen

12

Oh, my God, who is that fine-ass brother at the bar? was the only question I had as I walked through the club. If I could get him in my VIP room it could be the perfect eye candy for those housewives who came to the club. *Let me see what magic I can make happen.*

I walked to the end of the bar. It was early in the evening so it wasn't crowded yet. I got the bartender's attention. "Hey, Kim, can you send that guy at the end a drink on me?"

She laughed. "That's so funny; he was just askin' 'bout yo' ass. What you want, top shelf or beer?"

I was surprised that he was asking about me. Shit, I was still in jeans, a razor-torn tee, hair in a bun and little makeup on. "Whateva he drinkin'."

"He ain't drinkin'. He sucking on air." Kim chuckled.

"Even better. Give him top shelf and tell him to met me in the VIP room in five and he can ask me all the questions he wants." I smiled walking off toward the dressing area.

I looked in the mirror to make sure all my slits on my T-shirt were exposing what I wanted. I undid my bun and used my fingers to sweep my hair to one side. I put a quick and loose fishtail braid in. I licked my lips and applied some more lip gloss to shine them up. After taking a last look in the full-length mirror I headed to the VIP room.

I walked out the dressing area and headed to VIP pass the bar. I saw someone standing by the door. He started to walk toward me.

"Are you Carmen?" he asked with a pleasant smile.

"Yes, I am. I heard you was askin' 'bout me. What can I help you with?" I got closer and the smell of his cologne drove me nuts—in a good way.

"Yes, I was."

"Are you interested in the VIP room? Or is there something else you may be interested in?" I asked in a low whisper in his ear. The side of my cheek touched his and my body was close to his. I put my hand on his chest to feel his pecks. They were big, but not too big.

"Can we go inside?"

"Umm, yeah, sure why not, but you haven't even told me your name."

"Wayne. I shouldn't be worried 'bout being in the room alone with you, right? I mean you ain't gonna hurt me are you?" He had to be joking with me.

"Do you want to get hurt? I mean, I think I could handle tying you up," I said with a huge smile. I turned to the door and punched in the code to open the door.

There was something about this guy that had me mesmerized. I didn't care if he had money, a wife, five kids, or a girl. I just knew I had to have him. His body was fine, but his face was even better. Light eyes, good hair, light complexion, tall enough for me, and his upper body felt like power under my hands. There was only one thing that would make this go left: a six-inch dick. No matter how good you look, if your cock couldn't hold up to your looks then he might as well hand over all the money if he wanted anyone by his side. I had to find out.

"Nah, I don't like to get hurt. I do better with love," he said moving closer to me.

"So tell me, why were you asking about me?" I was shocked that he didn't even look around the room at all the whips, chains, and the pulley system straps hanging from the ceiling. He didn't even bother to look up. I didn't know if that was just because he had no clue or was he really focused on me.

"I was actually just tryin' to get to you." His body was now close enough that we could kiss.

I never wanted someone so bad. I'd already decided he was going to get some; why should I make him wait for it? His scent and the dirty thoughts in my mind made me want him even more.

"Is that right?" I placed my lips on his. He quickly wrapped his hands around my ass cheeks.

He slipped his tongue slowly into my mouth playing with my tongue. I hadn't kissed like that in a while. It was like a first boyfriend kiss. The passion he showed made me want to rip my pants off. I passed my hand over his crotch and there was more than six inches and he wasn't totally hard.

"So, Carmen, let me ask you a question: what does someone have to do to get in this VIP room?"

I stepped back immediately making sure there was enough space for me to slap him if I needed to. "You better not be no fuckin' pimp cause I don't tolerate those types at all. I'll get yo—"

"Carmen, I'm not. Actually I don't have tolerance for those types either. My mission here was about you. The VIP room question was just that, a question out of curiosity. I apologize." He put his hand out.

I was thrown off a bit, but looking into those light eyes and holding his strong hand pulled me back in. I stuck my tongue into his mouth as his hands roamed my body. He rubbed the front of my jeans teasing my clit. He did the same with my breasts. I was feeling really hot suddenly and then I realized we couldn't do anything in here.

"Okay, okay, we must stop. This room is not the best place to have our first encounter. Look I'm going to be honest, I'm very attracted to you and would like very much for you to be my guest tonight; then maybe after I tuck in my last VIP guest we can pick up where we left off."

My pussy was already wet just thinking about his dick inside me. I was almost horny enough to cancel all the sessions and take him home to please me all night. But making money made me more horny so I wasn't going to cancel anything. It would be good to see how he acted when other females were throwing themselves at him.

"You sure you want to stop?"

I kissed him one last time and led him to the door. "Will you wait for me?"

"Damn straight. You can find me at the bar when you're finished." He kissed the back of my hand and headed to the bar.

I followed him and alerted the bartender that he was my guest and anything he wanted to put on my bill. "I'll see you soon," I whispered in his ear.

When I left the bar I walked straight into the dressing area and pulled aside two ladies who had it all. I told them that I had a special friend at the bar and they should treat him to all their tricks. They already knew I would hit them off at the end of the night with some bills. They both agreed as I pointed him out at the bar.

The night couldn't move any slower than it was. I kept looking at my watch every hour and checking the bar to make sure Wayne didn't leave. But those ladies had him occupied as I requested. It was finally two in the morning and my last VIP session just ended. It was time to have some fun. I walked into the dressing area and found the two ladies I enlisted to keep Wayne busy while I was taking care of business. I pulled out four hundred-dollar bills and handed them over to them.

I walked over to the bar and tapped him on the shoulder. "Are you having fun?"

"I will now," he said with a smile. He looked at me up and down.

My outfit was different from when he first saw me. I had my short black leather miniskirt on with my thigh high boots and a black silk, low-neckline top. It exposed my goods just enough for anyone to image their head between them.

"Well, let's go then."

He grabbed my waist and held me close for a few seconds. "You look so good. If no one was here I would lay you across this bar and give you every inch of me. Deep and hard," he whispered.

Instantly my nipples were hard and my pussy was hot. I stayed close to him and took his hand and placed it in his lap then I straddled him. His eyes widened when he realized I had no panties on. I leaned back a little and moved my hips in a slow circular motion as his fingers played with the inside of me. I could feel his stiffness beneath me and wanted him inside me.

"I want you now," I said as I nibbled his ear.

"Your pussy is so wet . . . I want to taste it. Will you let me?" His fingers kept moving in and out of me making me hotter with every poke.

"C'mon let's get out of here." I rose up and pulled him off the stool.

"Hey, no need to rush. I ain't leavin'."

We couldn't get out the club any faster. When we got outside my driver was already there. As soon as we got into the car I attacked him like a tiger that hadn't eaten in a week. I unbuckled his pants and pulled out his third leg. I climbed on top of him and took every inch he had in me. He was big enough and his rhythm was in sync with my every bounce. He exposed my breasts and sucked on my nipples causing me to climax way too early. I didn't want to stop.

"Oh, my goodness, this pussy is so tight and wet . . . mmmm . . . I'm gonna cum all in you, I hope you're protected."

"Don't worry, baby, cum all you want. I can't get pregnant." I bounced up and down on his stiffness and climaxed with him.

"Ahhh . . . damn, girl . . . this feels so good," he moaned.

"Wait 'til I get you alone, baby."

I climbed off of him and sat beside him. He fixed himself and buckled up pretty quickly. I guessed he wasn't used to someone watching. I didn't care who snuck a peek on the other hand.

"So where we goin'?" he asked.

"We going to the closest five-star hotel. Is that cool? I mean you don't need to tuck nobody in do you?" Not that it mattered if he did, but I couldn't be entirely disrespectful. At least if I'm asked, I can say I did, but it wouldn't fall on me.

"Oh, no, I'm not like most. No kids, wife, or girlfriend. Totally free and single. No one to check in with or check on. What 'bout you?"

"That makes it a whole lot easier. Well . . . have you heard of complicated?" I wanted to be truthful for some reason.

"Complicated? Does that mean you got a baby daddy in jail or somethin'?"

I laughed at the question. "No, baby, nothin' like that. More like a stalker that I made the mistake of fucking. Is that too complicated for you?"

"Nope, not at all, I'm okay with that for now. So tell me what else do you do besides host a VIP room?"

Is he really interested? Or does he just want more pussy? The questions in my head were making me second-guess him, but when I looked at his sweet face the doubt disappeared. I felt the car slow down. "We must be here."

"And where is here?" He opened the door and stepped out the car.

I followed him and told the driver I would call him in a few hours. I took his hand in mine and walked into the Four Seasons off the LIE. When we walked in I walked straight to the guest services desk and requested a one-bedroom suite with a bottle of champagne on ice. I started to reach into my purse, but Wayne stopped me. He reached into his pocket and pulled out a wad of cash. After peeling off a few hundred the hotel rep handed him a key card. Once we entered the elevator and the doors closed the fun began. I backed into a corner and pushed myself up on the handle railing around the elevator.

"You still want to taste it?" I set each foot on the railing, opening my legs wide.

He happily obliged my need. His strong tongue hit my hard clit with force causing a burst of goodness to seep out of me. Wayne sucked and flicked his tongue so well that my legs shook like shake hand weights. I was so weak when the elevator chimed at our floor. He picked me up and carried me down the hall to our room. When he put me down it was like my legs weren't there anymore. It felt so good; I hadn't had someone please me in a while. He opened the door and I slowly walked in dropping my purse on the floor.

I wanted to take control. I lay on the bed for a minute then finally I felt strength in my legs again. I stood up and there was a knock at the door. He walked over to the door and opened it.

"Room service, sir." The young man wheeled in a cart with a bottle of champagne in a bucket on ice.

"Thank you." He pulled out a bill from his pocket and handed it to him. Wayne took the champagne out of the bucket and popped it open. He poured two full glasses and walked over to me.

I was staring out at the lights of the city. He handed me a glass.

"I would like to make a toast. To new lovers and old friends," he said tapping my glass gently.

My eyes focused on his. No words were said; he simply removed my glass from my hand and started to kiss my neck. His wet, soft lips turned me on. He dropped to his knees and lifted my skirt. When his warm mouth covered my clit an instant jolt came over my body.

"Yes, baby, suck on this pussy . . . make me cum again." I held his head closer and it felt like my knees were about to buckle. I let go of his head. "My legs are about to give. You suck on it so good." I started to pull my shirt over my head and unsnapped my bra then threw everything to the floor.

"I got you." He stood up and scooped me into his arms and walked over to the bed. He gently put me down and removed my skirt.

"Keep my boots on," I insisted. There was nothing sexier than a woman naked with thigh-high boots on.

He stepped back from the bed, removed all of his clothing, and kicked off his sneakers. Looking at his fully naked body made me melt. His body was toned to the tee; six-pack abs and muscles well defined. He stood at the edge of the bed and stared at me.

"Your body is perfect. Beautiful round tits"—he slowly moved his fingers around my nipples—"tight, neatly waxed pussy"—he licked his fingers then glided them over my clit—"and you taste so sweet."

I opened my legs and exposed my clit with my fingers. I didn't have to say a word; he knew what I wanted. He tapped on my clit with his tongue with precision making me moan with every hit. The faster his tongue moved the more intense the feeling became.

"Yeah, get me there, baby . . . right there."

My climax was more powerful than in the elevator. I felt more like a woman than I ever did. After I came he climbed on top of me, spit into his hand, and rubbed his hard dick over me. I held my breasts together signaling him where I wanted him first. As he stroked between my tits I teased the tip of his cock with my mouth.

"Oh, yes, hold them tighter and keep your mouth open . . ." His strokes became faster.

I let my breasts go and took his cock into my mouth. He was huge and I gagged on him like a newbie. I couldn't stand the gagging fits I was having so I pushed him off of me and climbed on top of him. I slowly allowed every inch of him to enter me then I went buck wild on his ass. I spun around and bounced, I did a split and bounced, basically I turned out every trick I knew to get him to moan like a bitch. It worked because when he came his scream was so loud the front desk called to make sure everything was okay.

After both us fucked and sucked each other into the early hours of the morning, we were exhausted, too tired to even call room service for breakfast. We lay there in each other's arms, him running his fingers over my head and me circling his nipples on his chest.

"Is it crazy that I feel connected to you when we only met yesterday?"

"Is it crazy that I feel the same way?"

I loved Daniel, but he was always going to be in my life no matter what. I had accepted that, but my wants and needs had changed. I wanted more than a man who showed up when I was in trouble or every other week. I wanted a man I didn't have to travel to see if I needed a hug or a late-night kiss. I was growing tired of all the time I spent at the club to all the time I waited to see him. Our relationship was open; he did his thing and when I did mine no feelings were hurt. Now I wanted a closed one—no, I deserved one.

"No, it's not. So tell me what do you do?"

"I dabble in a little of everything. Construction, cloth-ing, modeling, even the restaurant business, but I want to be able just to relax and settle down. Find a woman who can fulfill my every need and desire." His words almost brought me to tears; it was the same thing I wanted—to settle down.

"Hmm, that sounds good. I'm tired of the running around myself. The same ol' people with the same ol' shit. It's the same thing no matter how you look at it."

"So you never told me what else you do besides host a VIP room. Just don't tell me you're married. I don't think I'm ready to let you go." He kissed my forehead softly.

I looked up at him and stared into his light eyes—he was genuine. I wanted to tell him everything I ever did up to now, all the wrong and all the right. I felt that true un-conditional love did exist and it was possible for someone like me. I kissed his lips and lost myself in his passion. He rolled on top of me and I could feel him growing. He kissed on my neck down to my breasts and slowly entered me. With every stroke he kissed me and never took his eyes off mine.

We didn't fuck like deprived convicts. Everything was slow and every sensation was felt between us. His touches summoned feelings I always knew I had as a woman. I didn't want to lose these feelings. I closed my eyes and held him close loving all what he gave me.

Cindy

13

A few weeks passed and everything was looking good; I got the place, the crew, the girls, and we already shot two videos. The funny thing was I never knew how big this could really be. I just thought of having some sex lines and every so often having a show via the Web, but Daniel had showed me a projection screen of ideas and plans. At first trusting Carmen was a risk, but I had to take it or else me and Sherry would be combing the streets for hoes. Thank goodness we weren't because, honestly, I didn't know if I could handle it.

After talking to Daniel at least three times a week about the business he allowed me to grow and develop my own ideas and new goals. Sometimes it felt as if I was a pain in his side but every time he came to town he made sure to see me. A couple of times I met him at his hotel, but when my uneasiness became visible I made it clear that this was a business relationship and my intentions weren't beyond that. He understood and never crossed the line.

I just wished that Wayne would reach out to me. It'd been weeks since I last spoke to him. I called him but it kept going to voice mail. His stuff was packed and ready for him to pick up, but he never came to get any of it. I just hoped he wasn't up to his old tricks. I wanted him to realize this was a way out, a permanent way to stay out of jail and skip out on an early death.

I asked Sherry if she heard from him and she hadn't so I was kind of worried. I picked up my phone from the nightstand and dialed his number. It rang a few times before I finally heard his voice.

"Hello."

"Wayne, are you okay? Where have you been? I've been calling you, leaving messages, texting you, why haven't you answered me? What have you been doing?" I paused for a minute realizing that my rapid fire might cause him to buck. I quickly added in a calm voice, "Look, I just wanted to see if you was okay. I was worried, that's all."

"Hmm, yeah, I'm good. What's the deal with you?"

"I got everything I needed and even shot two videos already. Got a contract and everything. What's up with you?"

"Actually, I'm tryin' to make something happen. I gotta wait on some niggas to hit me back about some shit."

"Where you staying . . ." I cut myself off realizing I shouldn't have asked that. I didn't want him to feel that it was all good again with me.

"One of my boys, why you ask?"

"Wayne, I want to hire you for a Web show. It's easy money and it involves sex, two of your favorite things." I closed my eyes and said a silent prayer hoping he would say yes.

He didn't answer right away. I didn't want to be pushy, but I didn't want him to feel like I threw him to the side. I still wanted to help him. I felt obligated to throw him a bone since I wasn't with him to make sure his ass wouldn't end up on a cold slab or behind bars.

"Wayne, you heard me?"

"Yeah, a'ight I'll do it, just tell me where and when."

"Okay, I will. Wayne, I need you to show up, okay."

"Yeah, don't worry I got you. Besides I want to see what you got goin' on with this thing."

"Cool, so I'll have Sherry call you."

"Cindy, you still fuckin' with that dude Daniel?"

"Yeah, who you think's getting me all the contracts and meetings? He's been really helpful with everything."

"Yeah, I'm sure he has," he said hinting Daniel didn't help because he wanted to.

"Stop being jealous, he's really a cool dude. You should really talk to him. He could probably hook you up full time as a porn star. I know you wouldn't mind that and you get paid. C'mon, Wayne, don't tell me you wouldn't want that. Legit money, you wouldn't have to live that day-to-day life anymore." I didn't want to lecture, but I had to put it in his head that he could change for the better.

"A'ight, I'll meet him if you come too. Maybe you're right, this day-to-day shit ain't workin' no more, and the other day I almost got locked up 'cause I had two bands on me. Ain't that some bullshit? But listen to the craziness, I was in a fuckin' store."

"You see that's what I'm talkin' about, Wayne, shit like that. You need to be able to not feel like you gonna be locked up 'cause you got a wad of cash on you. Okay, so I'll call him and set something up. Talk to you soon." I pressed end quickly.

It was a relief to hear that he was okay. There was only one problem: talking Daniel into meeting him again. Last time didn't go over too well and I didn't want this time to go wrong or Daniel might not fuck with me at all again. I had to call him to feel everything out.

I scrolled through my call log and called the last number he called me from. He never kept the same number for some reason. His number changed like I change my underwear.

"Hello," he answered.

"Hey, Daniel, are you busy right now? I wanna talk to you about something."

"Cindy, you know I'm here for you. What's up? Did the lawyers send over the contract? Did you provide the info for the other LLC?"

"Yeah, I'm all good with that. I wanted to talk to you about Wayne."

"Cindy, you know I don't get caught up in anyone's personal shit. If you need to use any lawyers for him go ahead, just make sure you personally take care of it." He sounded a bit annoyed.

"No, it ain't like that. If he was locked up I would leave his ass there, trust me." He didn't know I was lying. "I want you two to meet because I was thinking of using him in one of these Web cam shows. I mean there's lots of shit for the men to get off, why not the ladies? They want to get off too. And I think if it does well, we can move ahead with a video special. If we promote it right we could have a star in the making."

"Cindy, just 'cause he can fuck you well doesn't mean he can do it on camera just as good."

I wasn't feeling that answer. "Daniel, let's be clear, I used to fuck him. Second, I don't speak about what or who is doin' me. Third, I want him to have a job, that way he won't be plotting and scheming to take it from me. Can you feel where I'm coming from now?" I wasn't holding back tone.

"Okay, so why you ain't say that shit first? Cindy, you should know by now that I don't like being taken around the mulberry bush before you poke me in my ass. Look, honestly, I don't care about meeting him. I just don't want the same bullshit as before. If he respects me as a man I can do the same. That's what men do."

"Thanks, Daniel. When are you in town?"

"I'll be in town later tonight. Why don't we meet at the Four Seasons in Midtown Manhattan? Do you know the address?"

"Yeah, I know where. I'll see you at seven."

"Sounds good, see you then."

The phone call ended and I felt better about the entire situation. It should be smooth as long as Wayne kept his mouth shut. I sent a text to Wayne letting him know where and when. I just hoped he would respond. If he didn't then I could say I tried my best and wouldn't try again. For sure he would be left alone. He had five hours to hit me back, but knowing him he'd probably just show up.

I walked into the Four Seasons restaurant and spoke to the hostess, "Hi, I should have a reservation under Daniel for a party of three. I don't know if I'm the first to arrive."

"Actually no, someone just arrived. Please follow me," the petite woman said.

She led me to a corner table farthest from the door. I knew it; Wayne was seated at the table talking to the waitress.

"Here you are, miss," she said pulling out my chair.

"Hey, Wayne." I kissed him on the cheek before I sat down. "Thank you," I said to the waitress.

"Hello, my name is Susan. I'll be your waitress for the night. Can I start you off with a cocktail?"

"Yes, please, I'll take a vodka and cranberry with a splash of lime. Thanks."

"I understand we're waiting for another person. I'll give you some time to look over the menu. I'll be right back with your drinks." She placed a menu in front of me.

"What you got to drink?"

"A bottle of Cîroc," he said with a smile.

"Now why would you order a bottle of it? You know you not gonna drink all that shit in one sitting. And you sure as hell can't take that shit in a doggie bag. Wayne, please don't show out. I want you to do good and this opportunity is something I don't want you to fuck up. I just don't want you to fuck it up for me. You hear me."

"Yeah, I hear you."

I saw the hostess leading Daniel to our table.

"Please, Wayne, I'm begging you."

Daniel reached the table; I stood up to greet him. He kissed me on the cheek and put his hand out to shake Wayne's hand. "Hello, I'm Daniel McConnelly."

Wayne stood up and formally introduced himself. "Hey, I'm Wayne Dixon. Sorry about our first encounter, but I wasn't informed of your dealings with Cindy that's all. But that's all cleared up now."

"All right, I respect that. I do know what surprises can do to a man. So now that we got that straight, let's talk about you getting into this business. Cindy told me a little about her plans, but let me hear from you."

"Yeah, definitely." He looked to me. "Maybe Cindy would be the better one to explain. I'm just a body ready to work."

The waitress came by and put our drinks on the table. She took Daniel's drink order and he told her to come back for our dinner orders.

"Well, I was thinking that you do some Web cam shows and then we can move into the video sales. I think we have to see how well you perform under the lights."

Wayne almost choked on his drink.

"Perform under the lights?" He looked confused.

"Yes, because fucking for pleasure is totally different when it comes to fucking for money. I can't begin to tell you how many guys think it's easy but once they get under those lights and cameras it's limp dick central. That can't happen if we're trying to make you a household name. I hope you understand that and don't take it personal." He looked to me as if I cared.

"Nah, not at all; I understand. But we won't know 'til I get under those lights. So I think if we try it out now while the company is still tryin' to find its fans it won't hurt. Let's talk 'bout the money."

There he was getting ready to turn it up. I guessed he didn't realize I would be the one paying him.

"You can talk to Cindy about that. You're not coming in under my company. You'll be doing scenes for Cindy's brand. I'm sure she'll come up with a fair deal." I noticed he kept looking at his watch. Suddenly his phone buzzed on the table. I saw that it was Carmen calling him. "Listen, I'll be right back." I watched him walk out the restaurant.

"So, Cindy, let me hear it. What's the offer?"

"Wayne, please, you'll get what I give you. Trust me it'll be fair." I wasn't really bothered with Wayne at the moment. I wanted to make sure Daniel was okay. I knew he was helping Carmen, but it seemed that she called him every time we got together. I wasn't jealous, but I was sure he could brush her off until our meeting was done. He was a busy man, but when he was with me I wanted his full attention.

"A'ight, I'll trust you, but I thought this dude was gonna make me some kind of star or somethin'. Seems to me that he leaves everything for you to handle. Tell me somethin' else." He poured another glass of Cîroc, then continued, "How does Carmen come into play in all of this?"

"Carmen?" I looked at him a little funny. Why was he asking about her? Did he know something I didn't?

"Yeah, wasn't she the one who introduced you two?"

"Yeah, but the only thing she does is supply girls if I need them. Most of the time I just hold auditions and pick

from there, but sometimes those girls back out at the last
minute. I call her and, poof, a girl appears so I don't lose
the day of filming."

"I see. So basically she the pimp, huh?" He grinned.

"Wayne, I think you still confused. This is legit, ain't no
pimp shit happening." A few minutes had already passed
and Daniel hadn't returned yet.

"So where yo' boy went to?"

"I'm about find out. Here's the waitress." When the
waitress came to the table I inquired about the man who
was sitting with us. She handed me a note.

> Sorry, Cindy, but somethin' came up. I've
> taken care of the bill so please have a lovely
> dinner on me. I will call you tomorrow.
> Daniel

"I knew it; that motherfucker jumped the boat and left
me with the fuckin' bill. I told yo' ass he was too good to be
fuckin' true. What man throws money into an investment
when he don't even know you? I don't know, Cindy, but we
gonna see if he's really who he say he is."

"Wayne, stop hatin'!" I showed him the note. By the
look on his face I knew he felt stupid. "Yeah, you still think
there's a problem? Don't worry, you don't have to take care
of the bill. He handled that as he was supposed to. I think I
lost my appetite. You can have dinner by yo'self!" I got up
from the table and walked out the restaurant.

I hated the way Wayne always tried to turn a positive
into a negative. They always said misery loves company
and that he was—miserable. He never wanted anything
for me that was good if it didn't help him. I was going to
give him what he wanted only because I wasn't like him.
I always looked out for him no matter what the situation
was. I was sure he was just jealous that someone other

than him was providing me with a way out of the ghetto life I was used to.

At that moment I realized Wayne wasn't my responsibility anymore. I would put the offer on the table and it would be up to him to make the decision. I couldn't force him. I only hoped that he would make the right choice to follow my lead.

Wayne

14

It'd been months and Cindy got the business off the ground. It was a snowball effect; everything happened quicker than she planned. This dude gave her a huge advance, schooled her to the industry, and even provided an outlet for getting girls from time to time. I didn't believe all of it, at first, because there was no way anyone could be that lucky to just meet someone like that.

My first encounter with Daniel wasn't the best, but on our second I put my assumptions to the side and my pride. He didn't say much because he left, which was kind of weird. After our meeting I didn't bother to inquire anymore about him only because from what I was seeing he was on the up-and-up. I asked some of my peoples and they all said he was legit. Never fucked with the underground worlds—drugs or prostitution.

With that information I left everything alone and started to work with Cindy. She kept me busy doing scenes or sometimes directing them every time I wanted to expand my budding career and talk to Daniel about ideas I had. I felt like a minion. So one day I flipped out on her and demanded another meeting with Daniel or I wasn't doing another scene.

I knew I was valuable after my first Web show crashed her site. I made her think she did me wrong, played the trust card, and the guilt of breaking up with me. I dug into her deep about wanting me to do right and becoming the man she could depend on without giving me a piece of the business. Of course she paid me for the work I did and I also got finder's fee for the girls I brought to her, but that didn't matter. I felt like she was keeping shit from me in the beginning and this dude was a constant topic. "Daniel showed me this. Daniel got me this connect."

When my nagging became a problem with her production she finally set up another meeting. When we met this time, I felt out of place, almost like it was their first date. At the time me and Cindy was going through the motions; break up to make up. Daniel acted as if he didn't know our personal business, but he knew. His charismatic and chivalric behavior made sure Cindy was aware of it. I didn't want him to know she was *my* meal ticket, but I was sure he figured that out by now. He had some arrogance to him; he kept throwing out what he had and what he would produce for Cindy, and how my career could be catapulted to the big leagues.

I remembered, he talked Cindy's head off about how much my scenes would make if she made them a little more risqué. He told both of us that underground porn was where a lot of money could be made. Of course he wanted to guide her because he didn't want her to fall in with the wrong people. From their conversation it seemed like he and Cindy had a lot more in common than just business. His game was good, but there was something that kept nagging at me. There's no way he was doing this for nothing. There had to be a catch.

After dinner I noticed how he made sure to let me know that he "got the check"—was that because Cindy said something to him about our last dinner meeting? Shit, we was at a five-star restaurant in Lower Manhattan; I sure as hell wasn't getting the check no matter how much money I was making.

When me and Cindy were alone I voiced my opinion to her again; she copped an attitude as if I shouldn't meddle in her business. I left it alone and concentrated on my new career. I stopped fucking Cindy completely after I signed the contract. I figured it was time to be true to her and let her go. Although if she approached don't think I wouldn't be ready to please. To tell you the truth Carmen had me pretty busy so I couldn't fuck with her even if I wanted to.

After meeting Carmen and spending the next two days with her, she told me all about Daniel. I had to come clean about my relationship with him as well. To my surprise Carmen was about her money like I was. She told me that Daniel helped her out with some loans she had acquired through some not-so-common banking methods. I asked her flat out if she was fucking him; she said no, but I didn't believe her.

Again, there was no way a man was giving up that type of money unless they were fucking them. In Cindy's case, I knew she wasn't fucking him, but it sure looked funny when they sat together at our last meeting. There was something Carmen wasn't telling me about Daniel, but I ignored it. I continued fucking her, but I told her we couldn't let Daniel or Cindy know because it would just cause a mess that neither one of us wanted—we both wanted our cake to eat.

Now that she got her sex lines and Internet porn making her some real money she had tunnel vision: her business making as much money was her only focus. Cindy continued to highlight me in live Web cam shows exposing all different sexual tricks. She made me sign a contract satisfying both my hungers: money and pussy. My fear was the commitment I had to make in order to get fed and to keep her close.

Cindy put Sherry in charge of the day-to-day operations and making sure all sex lines and Web sites were
active without any problems. All of the monies generated
were directly deposited into Cindy's business account.
Sherry only had access to a limited amount of money
and I had none. I had some ideas for the business and
sure wasn't going to spend my money to put it in motion.
Cindy sure wouldn't let my name near any of her money.
I got handed a check like everybody else.

Lately it'd been me and Sherry hanging out. Surpris-
ingly we actually got along after me and Cindy broke
up. I guessed she was just looking out for her friend
and I couldn't hold that against her. I mean if she didn't
understand I needed free rein on what my definition of a
relationship was, that was her problem not mine. Since
she'd been working with Cindy for the past seven or eight
months I saw her more than Cindy. I didn't even care
when she saw me naked or doing my thing on camera. It
actually helped me act even better. The thought of Sherry
watching my every move made my dick even harder. She
wasn't my type, but I sure would fuck her in a heartbeat.
Maybe getting to her that way would make Cindy jealous,
causing her to entrust me with more responsibility.

I knew Cindy had a trip to Europe for a few days to
finalize a distributor in Europe for the kinky sex acts
she'd been trying to shoot. I had the feeling I could make
a move on Sherry at that time, but I had to be sure of what
I was going to gain in return. For now I had to get to the
Jersey to meet up with Sherry.

"Yeah, baby, that's it lick that spot . . . faster . . . ooohh
yeah, I'm cumming for you . . . mmmm . . . get all of it or
mama gonna have you lick it off the floor," said a tall, slim,

dark-skinned woman dressed in a tight, shiny leather Catwoman-like costume with all the essential parts to every man completely exposed. Her six-inch knee-high boots made her even sexier. It fit her like a glove; every entry was penetrable. Her breasts were perfectly perched. Her pussy and ass were oiled and prepared for pleasure— naughty or wickedly good.

There I was turning my fantasy into reality. My body was oiled, buck naked, kneeling in front of her sucking all she had to give me. My hands were tied behind my back loosely. I can't wait to get my hands on her. I'd make sure she wouldn't be able to walk properly after I'm through.

"I'm gonna untie you now, but don't touch me and stay on your knees. You hear me?" she commanded.

I was dying to stick my ten inches deep into her. I basically slipped out of the rope around my hands; she only made the movements for the camera shot. I waited patiently for my next command.

"Now . . ." She stood directly in front of me. I had to fix my posture so my face was perfectly positioned in front of her bare flesh. She put each of her feet on either side of me as if she was going to straddle me. I positioned myself to rest my bare ass on the bottom of my feet.

My face lit up. She lowered herself onto me, but not all the way. I thrust my hips a bit, she slapped me across my face.

"I didn't tell you to move." She slapped me again a little harder this time around.

I smiled for the camera. Her opening was only allowing a portion of my head inside of her. Her wetness made me harder and my eagerness to fuck the shit out of her was building rapidly. I didn't know how much longer I could hold myself back.

"Don't move or you won't get mama's good stuff." She opened her legs wider and placed her hands on her knees. She lowered herself slowly swallowing all of me finally.

"Yes . . ." I screamed out. Her pussy was tight; it felt like her walls had clamps holding my dick inside her.

Quickly she rose to her initial position of only the tip of me in her and slapped me across the face. "I didn't give you permission to speak."

I hated these types of scenes. Sherry was supposed to make sure it was me being the aggressor instead of the submissive. As much as I liked a good slap, every now and again, this chick wasn't about to turn me into her bitch.

She wrapped her fingers around my neck and squeezed. I moved my neck back a bit to let her know her grip was tight enough. Soon after, she bounced up and down taking only inch by inch of my hard rod inside her. Her moaning became louder after the first six inches. I placed my hands on her hips and forced her down all the way. She didn't stop me.

"Yes, fuck me harder." Her grip around my neck got tighter. "Fuck me!"

While she was choking me, I was slamming her down on my hard cock making her feel every inch of me. "Yeah, take it, bitch," I whispered.

Quickly her fingers loosened around my neck and she started to rise. I was confused. Why would she get up? Then my eyes got a glimpse of what was behind her—a tantric sex chair with straps on the side. I loved these chairs. They were made specifically for a woman's body. There were two points of height on this chair for a precise fucking position—raised at the head and the middle so the woman's ass was perched up.

"Strap me up and fuck me like you want to," she said with a smile.

I did what I was told with a happy grin like a kid in a candy store. After strapping her to the chair I stuffed my dick in her mouth to suck. I saw the mouth gag on the floor. I pulled my dick out her mouth, picked up the gag and fixed it to her mouth. With her hands tied to the side of the chair and her feet tied to each side. She was about to feel the heat; unfortunately her screams would be muffled so I wouldn't be able to know how much pleasure she was loving. It didn't matter anyway; I was going to bust my nut and more.

I fucked her from behind making sure to return all the slaps she gave to me in the beginning of this scene. She was going to learn I don't like chicks slapping me in my face making me look like someone's bitch. I smacked her round oiled ass gently at first, but with each thrust they became harder leaving red marks on her butt. After a while I pulled out and shoved the head of my dick into her asshole.

Her head turned quickly and I could see her struggle a bit to try to stop me. The way I saw it she was paid for the day and she requested that I fuck her the way I wanted. Pushing all ten inches into her tight little asshole made me want to cum quick. I pulled out to stop the flow of goodness. "Oh, damn, your asshole's so tight . . . mmm mmm mmm." I lowered my head and licked her from behind to make her forget the pain I just inflected. I didn't think she liked the fact that I was in control—too bad, I liked it. I saw Sherry smiling at me when I raised my head; I could tell she liked the show I was putting on. Secretly, I believed she got off on watching my moves.

After licking her bare lips and finger fucking her asshole she was ready. I got back into position. I played with her clit with my left finger while I stroked my cock with my right hand awaiting her climax. Once she did I entered her asshole and pumped fast and hard. At one point I could feel her back her ass up a little bit; that's when I grabbed each of her ass cheeks in my hands. If she didn't know my strength before she was going to know by the time I was finished. As hard as I could I rocked her back and forth on my stiff Johnson making sure I spread her ass cheeks so the camera could get close-up shots of my entry.

She felt so good to me, nothing like anyone else I ever had. I busted my nut all over her face then I pissed on her—on some R. Kelly shit. I didn't like how I was made a bitch. She was still tied up and gagged; there was nothing she could do. All she did was buck like a horse. It was actually funny. *I gots to get a unedited version of that shit.* My dirty thought produced a big grin on my face.

"Wayne, what the fuck you doin'?" Sherry yelled out.

"What, you can't use none of that?" I shouted back as I walked toward the bathroom.

"You didn't have to piss on her! Shit, what the fuck is Daniel going to say? This girl was one of his not ours. You so fuckin' stupid I swear." I could hear her screaming at me.

"Daniel? What the fuck he gonna do? He's the one pushin' Cindy into some next shit. And got me doin' some crazy shit to make it work!" I said loudly hoping she heard me. I walked into the bathroom and thought how Sherry was such a hypocrite. *Daniel ain't nobody, he can get broke down the same way a bitch do. Sherry is always smiling when his name is mentioned but as soon as she's with me the complaints are overwhelming. How his girls always skinny, hairy as shit, and their teeth yellow or jacked the fuck up. But yet as soon as Cindy starts her "Daniel said this," "Daniel said that" bullshit she got nothing but ideas and strategies on how he could help. I ain't even gonna think 'bout all the bullshit she tries to feed me half the time.*

There was a bang at the door.

I flinched. "Who the fuck—"

"Open the fuckin' door, you asshole!" a squeaky voice yelled continuing to bang on the door. "You open this door now. Wait until I tell Daniel. He's going to have your head!"

I opened the door quickly. I was still naked but I didn't care. I smiled at her. "Don't threaten me, bitch. Daniel don't run shit here, and definitely don't run me. That's the type of shit you got paid for, bitch. Get the fuck over it." I stared at her for moment then brushed passed her to see Sherry heading my way.

All I wanted was a shower and some decent food. I didn't want any bullshit.

"Wayne, explain to me what the fuck you tryin' to do? That shit was not a good fuckin' look. Facts." Sherry folded her arms across her chest.

"Sherry, please, you and I both know that shit is what Cindy wants now. So what! Did I take it too far for you?" I smiled at her.

"Can you put on a fuckin' towel or something please? Shit." She looked down the hall to see if someone was there. "Hey, Diana, bring a towel please before you head out for lunch."

"I don't need a towel. You see me like this all the time."

"I ain't gonna talk to you lookin' like this."

Diana soon appeared with a towel in hand. Sherry took it out her hand and shoved it in my face. Sherry waited for everyone to leave before she started to mouth off again.

"Put it on."

"No." I shoved her hand away; it dropped to the floor. "C'mon, man, I don't have time for this shit."

"What do you think Daniel's gonna say? You think pissin' on one of his girls is okay? Why you wanna go fuck shit up when we all gettin' money?"

"Why you so shook?" Sherry was supposed to be from the hood, know a game when she saw one. She didn't know Daniel was sneakier than me.

"Ain't nobody shook of that motherfucker. I just don't want yo' ignorant, jealous, attention-needy ass to fuck up this money for any of us including yo' dumb ass."

"Why you even in my face, Sherry? Throw that bitch another two bands. I bet you she won't have nothin' to say but when can she do the next one. I'm so tired of this shit. You don't even know what you doin' or how much power you really got!"

Sherry rolled her eyes. "Tired of what? Tired that every time you try to run shit you fuck it up? Tired that Cindy leaves you to your hoes while she's off doin' shit that matters? Tired of—"

"Sherry, you lucky I don't hit females no more. 'Cause, trust me, yo' delicate face would be black and blue. Then *you* would really be tired." I laughed at her disrespect.

Sherry turned silent all of a sudden. Stunned I expected.

"Why you so quiet? What, you got nothing to say now? I ain't gonna hit you. Say what you gotta say." I folded my arms on my chest and got into a firm stance with my nuts swinging in the wind.

Sherry looked around then at me up and down. She placed her hands on her hips and stepped a little closer to me—her breath was Bubblelicious-scented.

"Wayne, you ain't shit and will never be shit. Don't get fuckin' mad 'cause yo' ass couldn't make it happen. You actually lucked out, 'cause now you making money for shit you been doin' on the sly. I know you ain't tryin' to go back to robbin' flashy motherfuckers you see the clubs or whorin' yo'self out to pay yo' way. What Cindy gave you actually made yo' life relevant and whole."

Her words hit me like a ton of bricks. "Hold on, who you think you talkin' to?" *She better watch her mouth.* I didn't care that she was right. I knew slapping a gift horse in the mouth was bad karma.

"Ain't nobody else 'round!" she snapped.

"Sherry, *you* ain't shit. I thought me and you had an understanding: you don't put yo' two cents in my movement and I won't worry 'bout yours. You act like I'm against all this shit. I'm not stupid to fuck up something actually legit that could either put us on the good path or the shortcut to hell. And I'm all in. I don't see you showin' all that you got. Now you sayin' some off-the-wall bull-shit. I'm not in this shit to fuck bitches; I did that while I was with Cindy." I stepped back and rubbed on my dick a little then continued, "Bitch, even you want to fuck me. I see the way you look at me. I can have a new bitch every day if I wanted to without doin' this."

"Nigga, please." She pushed back on my chest with both her hands throwing me off my balance a bit. "Why would I want you? You ain't no real man. A real man would have provided for his, not allowed his fuckin' girl to make major moves."

"Oh, is that so? You know what I don't understand 'bout you and Cindy, y'all trust this dude Daniel an awful lot." I tilted my head back a little and cocked it to the side. I decided to pick up the towel and wrapped it around my waist.

"What the fuck you talking about? You crazy and insecure. What's a matter you mad 'cause you lost her? Or you just mad 'cause you can't get no more?" She batted her eyes and posed seductively.

This bitch is really trying to get on my nerves. Maybe she needed her eyes opened to this guy Daniel. Just because he talked a good game and showed a good game didn't mean he was a good person. I honestly didn't care about who she was fucking, but the thought of her seeing this guy when we was going through our shit wasn't sitting right with me.

"Got nothing to say, huh?" she taunted. "That's exactly what I mean. You can only control yo' dick. Everything else you suck at!"

She turned her back to me. She wasn't going to flee without my response. I reached for her arm and pulled her to me. I held her tightly and kissed her. I didn't know what to expect; if Cindy walked in it wouldn't look good of me. I didn't know if anyone would snitch on me or if Sherry would straight out slap the shit out of me. When my lips touched hers, it didn't take long for her to open her mouth and slide her tongue into mine. After a few seconds I think she realized where she was and pushed me away. My dick was ready to make her scream.

Suddenly the bathroom door opened and Daniel's girl, Cherry, stood there. I quickly backed up and made sure my towel was wrapped tightly around me. Her smooth chocolate skin glowed against the short stark white robe wrapped around her body. "Yo, umm . . . we gonna give you extra for that scene. I went overboard. My fault."

"I want a double day pay in cash, now. My day is over."

"It's only noon. We got to shoot as much as we can today. We rented the space for these scenes today and it's only for twelve hours. I can't get nobody on this short of a notice. Who the fuck I'ma get right now?" Sherry was not happy, but I was going to show her how to fix a problem smoothly.

"Sherry, pay her the double day in cash and let her go home. Matter of fact give her an extra band so she can tell Daniel how well we treated her." I stepped closer to Cherry and touched her face gently. Her reaction showed me that I was right all along—money will shut any chick up.

Sherry wasn't moving. She rolled her eyes.

"Why don't I call Daniel and get his opinion." Cherry started walking toward the staircase to the second floor of the house.

"Walk now, and you don't get shit," I shouted out to Cherry. My words paused her actions momentarily.

"This is all 'cause of yo' ass! You see—" Sherry started to scorn me.

"Shut the fuck up, and go get the fuckin' money! So she can go on her merry little fuckin' way. I'll handle gettin' somebody else." I started to walk to the bathroom to take a shower.

"You gonna call one of yo' skanks to do it?" Sherry's voice was different, as if a green-eyed monster spoke in her ear.

"Why not? I ain't even gonna take my regular fee. Just go get the money and I'll show you how to do this." I motioned my hands for her to go get the money. "Cherry, why don't you get dressed then come see me for yo' money." I walked into the bathroom and shut the door. With a smile on my face and a purpose I turned the shower on and got in.

Maybe there was a gain even if it meant screwing Cindy in the end. If I convinced Sherry that my ideas were good maybe she could get it started without me having to put up the money. And if I fucked her well enough I didn't think I'd have to convince her about anything.

Carmen

15

It'd been a few weeks since I'd seen Wayne. When I told him about Daniel and he told me about Cindy I didn't want anyone to know at first. But now, it was getting serious. He spent almost every night at my place since we met. Keeping our relationship on the low was the best because if Daniel would have found out it wouldn't be good.

I really liked him and I thought Daniel would understand why I wanted to be with him. He was stable and someone I could show the world that he was mine. My relationship with Daniel was always a secret. I learned to live with it, but now that I was secure in my body I wanted to come out of the darkness.

I loved Daniel, but the more I thought about the true Daniel it scared me. When I told him to make things happen for Cindy I didn't think he was going to answer her every beck and call. Every time we saw each other she called or he had to meet her somewhere about a contract. And lately it'd been happening on the regular.

I found out that he was flying her to Miami, L.A., San Francisco for business meetings. It made me want to act the fool, but I didn't only because most of my lifestyle was funded by him. You don't bite the hand that feeds you, but something had to change. He'd been questioning me on why coming to my place had been such a problem. It was easy to give him an excuse. I didn't know if he truly wanted to spend time with me or just wanted to keep up appearances.

I picked up my phone and dialed his number.

"Hey, baby," his said in a soft tone.

"Hey, can I come see you in L.A. next week so we can talk about a few things? I think I'm ready to take a break."

"Take a break? What do you mean?"

"I really don't want to talk about it over the phone."

"Well, baby, I'm sorry, but I can't . . . You know what, okay, but you have to fly out tonight and leave the next day. I have a lot of running around to do and can't be with you that long. If you leave tonight you'll be here in a few hours and we can talk over lunch. It's up to you."

"So if I want to see you I have to travel over four hours on a plane just to have a conversation over lunch. Daniel, I used to be number one in yo' life. It seems that something else has been occupying your time."

"Carmen, I don't need your drama on top of all the shit I'm dealing with."

"And what exactly are you dealing with, Daniel? You haven't told me anything, let alone seen me, going on a few weeks now. You were supposed to call me last week with the Swiss account number. Are you tryin' to renege on what we agreed to?"

"Why would I do that? I just think I've gotten a little over my head with some new friends of mine."

"Over your head? Daniel, what did you do? I set you up with the perfect person. Clean name, no convictions, nobody ever heard of her, new business where you can easily produce clean money. Is that not the case now?"

"Nothing, don't worry about it. I'll text you the account number in a few. There's something else . . . my relationship with Cindy is growing into something more than business."

My heart sank. We made it clear to each other that when our new relationships erupted into anything more we would be honest with each other. Now I regretted that agreement. It was clear that he was ready to move on, but I wasn't so sure about me. It was good with Wayne, but I still thought he had other intentions and wouldn't understand who I was truly.

"Hmm, I see. So, you're telling me this because . . . ?" I knew why he was telling me, but I needed to hear it from his mouth that he wanted to stray from our relationship.

"Because we both should be honest with each other. You and I both know I will never marry you or parade you around like my wife and you know why." He said the truth that I knew all along.

I was different. I wasn't the average woman, but there were things I knew about him that wouldn't sit so well with a few of our mutual friends. He knew I would never out him; except if he didn't give me what's owed to me I would have to out his ass with no shame.

"I knew it. All this time you've been rocking with me only because you had the options of both worlds. After all these years of coming to my rescue, suddenly I'm not worth it anymore. Daniel, why did you help me in the first place?"

"I helped you because I felt I had to."

"I have to go. I'll call you back." I hung up the phone; tears were building in my eyes.

I met Daniel as a client about ten years ago; I was sixteen and a young boy. I ran away from home at the age of fifteen because my family and friends wouldn't accept my way of life. How I wanted to live, how I wanted to dress, who I wanted to hang out with. It was hard. I stayed on the streets of Chicago for months until I met another runaway just like me.

His name was Stevie and was just like me at that time; he dressed as a female and acted as a female as I did. I thought I could trust him. I thought he was my friend. It turned out that I was put into a situation where the only escape was to sell my ass. I got turned out and trafficked across state lines to a madam that solicited sex for the freaky; it was any and everything allowed. I eventually met Daniel and he called for me every time he was in town. It was nice because he allowed me to be me. He was only a few years older than me and accepted me. I didn't know what he did and didn't care at the time.

After two months of seeing me almost every week, he told me I was leaving with him. I was ready, but was scared of the consequences. He told me he took care of everything and I didn't have to worry about anybody hunting me down. Unfortunately, that was not the case. He took me away without paying his tab in a sense. The madam who owned my ass was a person you did not fuck with. Her tie to every trick that was turned in DC was endless and her friends were those of high regard: judges, politicians, lawyers, etc.

The first year was fun, we were best friends. He provided a home, and anything else I needed. I never crossed the line of forcing my lifestyle on him. We had an understanding that if we were with friends I would definitely have to stay in check. No outlandish acts that would give away my true identity and definitely present myself as a female at all times. It wasn't hard at first because I stayed to myself most of the times, but when he wanted to go to tropical islands and sandy beaches it became apparent that stuffing my bra wouldn't work. After I told him and cried my eyes out he took me to Brazil. There I had every surgery to make me a full-fledged woman: chopped my nuts, inverted my dick, implants, cheek bones, jaw line, chin, lipo, and my hair implants. I received the entire work-up and walked out of Brazil a month later feeling and looking like a woman more than ever.

When Daniel saw me he couldn't recognize me. He took me into his arms and for the next four years we were each other's family, friend, and lover. He became my everything—my only thing. Until by mistake I overheard him on the phone talking about selling girls, paying off people, extorting people; it scared me and I made a conscious decision to leave before I ended up dead. I left and didn't look back.

After a few years of living on my own I dabbled in a lot of things, but selling my ass was never one of them. My niche was gambling. I was good at it and started playing games everywhere I could and running up tabs, too. I thought I had a good thing going until I walked into a high-stakes card game in New Jersey and Daniel was there to collect my debt.

It was more of a surprise to him to see me at that game. To my astonishment he embraced me and whispered how much he missed me. When the game got started he pulled me to the side and spoke to me about how much money I owed people and how I couldn't keep borrowing if I wasn't going to pay it back. When I asked how he knew who I owed money to, he gave me a look. It scared me.

I pleaded with him at first then put the waterworks on. He took me into his arms and held me bringing back all those great memories we had together. I fell into his life again willingly, but on my terms. I told him it wasn't the days of me not knowing; he would have to bring me into his entire world including the money. Within a year I was working out of Frank and Lou's club. Daniel set up the entire deal. I owed them a quarter of a million dollars in gambling debts. He made it look like I was paying off the debt, but in actuality I was getting more money on the side by recording all VIP sessions and selling them overseas and on the Internet. It also gave me access to females for Daniel's porn sites, which I got some money from too.

There was so much me and Daniel went through, I didn't know if I was truly ready to let him go. But I did know if he didn't give me the money he promised me there would be a problem.

Cindy

16

Life is good, I thought sitting at the bar in The Dead Rabbit, somewhere in the Financial District. This bar was trippy; most of the patrons were in suits and ties—preppy, young, and old. Sipping on a glass of Patrón Silver in my open-back black Prada dress looking like a call girl ready to date, I looked around and most of the ladies were in gray and dull black pantsuits. I didn't think I would ever do a nine-to-five like a normal person. It felt good not depending on anyone anymore, especially Wayne. He was never good for me and it took me long enough to see the light.

I wouldn't have imagined myself here six months ago, let alone a year ago. I always knew there was money in this business, but producing it and being in it were two different things. It can all go the wrong way if you let it. I just had to make sure the right decisions were made and the right people were in place to handle it. Sherry I trusted, Wayne not so much. He's slick and always looking for an angle to gain, but I fixed that habit—pussy anytime, a flow of money on the regular, and a career that he doesn't have to work hard at.

It was funny how things worked out. Sherry didn't have faith, but I showed her that I was a woman of my word. With Daniel's help I was able to connect with up-and-comers trying to make a name for themselves in the industry and girls he sent my way. And with Sherry's hood friends always needing cash, it was opportunity at its best. Any female who didn't have her shit all out there like a glow stick was capable of doing it. Making this money and creating relationships for the long haul was my purpose.

Daniel was a breath of fresh air: a man willing to put in the work to get it. His skin color didn't bother me; it made me more curious. I wanted to know how it felt to be fucked by a white guy. Would he be big enough? Would he be satisfying or just weird? I had to know. If Daniel didn't want it after close to a year of knowing me I guessed it was never meant to be.

After being introduced to him we met up once every month for about six months straight. We mostly discussed business on the phone or e-mail at first. Then our meetings became more frequent, more personal, more relaxed; he was booking tickets for me to meet him in L.A. or wherever he was for just an hour or two. At first I thought he was trying to get into my pants, but if that was the case he would've tried in our first meeting, which was at his hotel room. But lately, the phone calls had been a little later and more questions about my likes and dislikes instead of business.

"Excuse me, may I join you?" Daniel snuck up behind me and whispered in my ear. His soft lips gently rubbed against my earlobe. It put a chill through my body. His cologne smelled refreshing and he was dressed to kill. His black-on-black attire fit for a James Bond scene instantly made me the envy of the room. When I looked around all the ladies had their eyes on us.

"Daniel, I already told you sneaking up on someone may just get yo' ass hurt." I put my serious face on.

He took a seat next to me and ordered a drink. "I'm sorry, but I just can't help myself around pretty women. It's my weakness."

"Oh, so all pretty women make you weak?" I repeated his words.

"Let me rephrase that . . . You make me weak. Let's make that clear," he said quickly removing his foot from his mouth.

I smiled. "So tell me again why I have to travel thousands of miles to do this deal instead of you making it happen?"

"This is a funny world. Everyone needs a face-to-face. They have to know who they are dealing with. And on top of that you want to get into the other side of this business—the closeted side." He arched his brow. "This distributor you'll meet is dependable and won't run with your product leaving you high and dry dealing with copyrights and breached contracts. Trust me—been there, done that, and learned from it. I'm just passing on the knowledge."

"And I appreciate that; now tell me what should I expect from this little meeting? You better not be sending me on some *Taken* shit either."

His head tilted and his eyes looked down. He didn't know what I was talking about.

"*Taken,* the movie."

He shook his head.

The reality of it all hit me: I was going to a foreign country to make a deal only worth $200,000. I only had a name, place, and time. According to Daniel if everything went well I would see double my money in less than a year. I couldn't even believe I was about to do this, but I trusted Daniel and he wouldn't push me in the wrong direction. "I think I need another drink." I held up my empty glass to the bartender and gestured for another drink.

Daniel was staring at me. His eyes were so tempting. I never thought about fucking anybody but Wayne before.

Now that Wayne made it clear to me that monogamy was not in his future I promised myself I would look for someone to love me the right way—a real man.

"Why you staring at me like that?" I asked as the bartender placed another drink in front of me.

"You're beautiful. I would really like to see you outside of business. I'm sure you've noticed lately that your trips have been a little less business." He smiled.

"Is that why you invited me here? 'Cause usually it's a restaurant or some kind of conference room." I looked around and laughed. I knocked back the rest of my drink and ordered another.

"Well, honestly I wanted to come clean and just put it out there. I like you and want more than what we have. Don't get me wrong, I like our relationship; that's why I want more. "

I smirked with dirty thoughts in my mind. *I wonder how much more can he handle.*

He laughed as if he already knew what I was thinking.

"So tell me, how solid is this distributor?"

"Okay, so you're going to let what I just said fly by?"

I grabbed a wedge of lime and sucked on it seductively. Secretly hoping his dick would become rock hard.

"Could you not do that? It's really distracting for me." He placed his hand on my knee and twirled his finger in circles.

It felt good. Maybe it was the glasses of Patrón I kept knocking back that made me more open. I should have stopped, but I didn't. I wanted him inside me. I refused to be sloppy and drunk fucking him. Sherry always said fucking the right man would secure the future of your dreams. He would die to give you the world and more. I had already made up my mind; he was going to get what he wanted—me. I knew mixing business with pleasure was always a no-no, but if it proved to be beneficial all around then there was no harm.

"Okay, enough distractions." I put the lime down and uncrossed my legs.

With a smile on his face he placed his hand just below the hem of my skirt, the middle of my thigh. "Cindy, this meeting will change your life. This business can either bring you a whole lot of money or it could destroy you—literally."

"You keep saying how important this is, but yet you're not telling me what I should do. Tell me what I should do." I turned my upper body to face the bar.

He moved a little closer to me. "Make the deal and come back home to me."

"Is that it?"

Daniel glided his finger on my bottom lip. My clit started to pulse. I wanted to do something crazy. I wanted to be bad.

"Yes, now enough business. Let's discuss what I mentioned before?" He waved to the bartender to come over. "Can we get a bottle of Dom at the table over there?"

"Sure. Should I start a tab?"

Daniel reached into his inside pocket of his blazer and pulled out his black Amex card. I bit my lip a little.

"Please put whatever the lady had on the card as well." He got off the stool and held out his hand. "Shall we?"

I took his hand in mine and grabbed my vintage Christian Dior clutch off the bar and followed him to the table. We sat in a dark corner, very secluded from the rest of the drinking crowd. I took a seat. The waitress arrived with our bottle and she handed me back my card that I gave the bartender earlier.

"Thanks. I just hope you don't think I owe you now." I chuckled and moved closer to him. I could smell his Clive Christian cologne. I knew that smell.

"Matter of fact I think you do . . ." He handed me a glass filled with champagne.

"And what's that?" I didn't want to drink another drop alcohol.

He raised his glass. "Here's to you owing me some of your time and attention."

I smiled and tapped his glass with mine. We sat there for close to two hours just talking about everything and anything. It felt good to have someone listen to me instead of someone pretending they did. After the second bottle he suggested we go to his hotel room to have some coffee and maybe something to eat. But I knew what was happening; I guessed he was trying to be a gentleman, but at this point I didn't care about chivalry. I did him a favor and made sure he understood I didn't play games. I stood up making sure I was extremely close to him. I did a quick wiggle and pulled down my thong. It dropped to my ankles. In a slow movement I stepped out of it, picked it up, and placed it in his hands. "I like to keep it spicy," I whispered into his ear.

The smile that came across his face was priceless and the bulge in his pants only got bigger.

"In that case I can't deny you. Let's get out of here." He tucked my thong into his pants pocket.

We walked out the bar and he whistled for a cab. He held my hand tight. His palms felt a little sweaty. Was he nervous like me? This was new for me. I never did anything like this before. A Yellow Cab stopped and he held the door open for me. I got in.

"Take me to the W Hotel. Do you know where it is?" he asked after getting in and closing the car door.

"Yes, I do," the driver answered.

My stomach was bubbling with nerves. I knew why. Daniel would be the second man I ever slept with. I didn't know if it was the right move, but it felt so good to have someone wanting me for a change. It was very different from someone needing me like Wayne.

His hands started to climb the inside of my leg then he moved in closer to kiss on my neck.

"Daniel, can I ask you one question?"

"You can ask me anything," he whispered.

"Why me?"

Suddenly he stopped kissing my neck and sat up. *Damn, did I ask the wrong question?* I thought.

"Why not you?"

I didn't know how to respond. I felt tears starting to build in my eyes. His question struck a chord.

"Cindy, if there's one thing you should know about me it's my love is never misleading. I generally don't mix business with pleasure. But you floored me. You have ambition, pride in what you do, you're sensible, intelligent, and definitely drop-dead gorgeous. Why can't I want you?"

"You can have anybody you want, why *me?*" I repeated myself.

"I have a confession . . ."

My teary eyes dried up real quick. It sounded like he was about to confess to some *Maury* show type shit. Instantly my body became defensive; my knees were touching and my ass was damn near hitting the door handle.

"Oh, my goodness, I think . . . Listen, the first time I met you wasn't the first time I saw you. I saw you dance at the club. It blew my mind. You worked that stage like a pro. All those men weren't just throwing money at you; there were many requests as to how many nights you danced, if they would be able to get a private room with you. It was crazy."

I was confused. "How did you see me dance? That's a hood club. I wouldn't think that was your type of scene. And what you talking about 'request me for a private room'? Was that a whorehouse?"

"You're right, it wasn't my type of scene, but it worked out I had to see the owners, Frank and Lou, personally. Let's say they were old friends. That little hole is well known for its extracurricular activities not shown on the menu. But we're getting off the subject. When I met you, honestly it was lust at first sight, but after a few months of talking to you almost every day my feelings have changed. It's not lust anymore; now I want to get to know you. Find out your likes, dislikes, take you here and there. I want to do things for you. Most women in your position would have already given it up and more, but you kept it straight. There was no hint of sneakiness and that's why I'm here now to stop the assumptions and let it be known."

"You're here," the driver said.

"Damn, that was quick," I blurted out.

"Have you changed your mind about coming up? You can take this cab home if you want. I don't want you to feel obligated to anything or me. I want you to want it too." Daniel opened the car door and stood at the driver's window. He reached into his inside pocket and pulled out a money clip, peeled off a fifty dollar bill, and handed it o the driver. He was about to close the door but I stopped him.

"I want it too." I stepped out the car and walked with him into the hotel.

The hotel was far from simple. The ceiling made me a little dizzy at first. It looked like waves in 3D form. The décor of the lobby had modern chairs and tables almost space-like. We walked straight to the elevator and even that look was spectacular; the lighting made it seem that we were about to step into a box of fire.

Once we were in the elevator it seemed that I killed the mood. He said nothing. I said nothing. My only question to myself was, *How bad did I fuck this up?*

He pulled out his key card and opened the door. Like a true gentleman he motioned for me to enter first. The suite was stark white with hints of color throughout. There was a living space with a sofa, a desk facing the huge window, TV screen mounted to the wall; it was straight out of a magazine. I wanted to walk around and check out the bathroom and bedroom, but I thought that would be too bold. I slipped my peep-toe pumps off, placed my clutch on the coffee table, and took a seat.

"I'll be right back. I want to get comfortable. If you want something to drink, please help yourself to the minibar." He walked toward the bedroom.

I sat there contemplating the situation. *Should I even do this? Maybe I should just leave. If I leave will he back out of everything?* I decided to stop second-guessing myself and just do me. I slipped out of my dress leaving on my pumps. At first lying on the sofa naked seemed like the obvious pose, but I decided to sit on the desk that was facing the window and put my foot on each arm of the chair; it wasn't the standard office chair either, more like something you would find at Ethan Allen furniture store.

"Umm . . . Cindy . . ." Daniel said as he was walking back into the room throwing a T-shirt over his head. He didn't see me yet.

"Daniel . . ."

His eyes first looked toward the sofa, but then they finally hit me. I was perched and ready for his taking. His eyes widened with a grin on his face. Daniel walked over and rested his hands on top of the chair.

"This is what I want," I said.

He moved the chair and caught my legs from hanging off the desk. His hands were soft; he squeezed the back of my thighs and pushed my legs up.

"This is nice . . ." He stared at my bare kitty and licked his lips slowly. "You ready for me?"

My pussy instantly became moist. All the sensations that came over my body made me want every part of his body on me. These were new feelings; I liked them. This could go all wrong or so right. I grabbed the heels of my pumps and pulled them back displaying all my goods. He bent his head down and slowly used his tongue to taste every inch of me. I let out a soft moan. His tongue moved slowly opening my slit, enjoying every drop of honey I spilled out. I let go of my heels and reached down to expose my pulsating clit so he would devour it. I wanted it bad.

"Yes . . . I didn't know you could make me feel this good . . . Damn, Daniel." He worked his tongue hitting my G-spot with precision. My entire body shook. I never experienced this feeling with Wayne.

"You taste so sweet . . ."

"Ahhh . . . you gonna make me cum . . . Oh, yes . . . lick that pussy." I used one of my hands to pinch my nipple. His tongue moved faster and my moans got louder. I was almost there.

"Yes, Cindy, cum . . . I want to taste it." He sucked all of my juices flowing out of me as I climaxed.

I was ready to be fucked. My legs were spread wide, my fingers were rubbing my hard nipples. I felt my body temperature rise and beads of sweat on my forehead. I just wanted him to fuck me; hopefully he wouldn't disappoint me.

Daniel stood up and I scooted to the end ready for his entry. With all the pornos I'd watched it was rare for a white man to be over seven, eight inches. I closed my eyes expecting nothing over the top.

I heard a crinkling sound. *It must be the condom,* I thought. He put the tip of his dick in me. I was so wet and ready, teasing me was not what I wanted.

"Fuck me, Daniel . . . stick your—"

Unexpectedly, he pushed himself deep into my flesh. It hurt to my surprise, but it was a good hurt. He was bigger than Wayne. I opened my eyes and saw him peering down admiring his strokes. He entered me again and again making my box hotter and wetter.

"Yes . . . fuck me faster . . . I want to cum all over your big cock . . ." He picked me up from the desk and continued to pump his hips. I bounced up and down until I came again. Suddenly my back was against the wall and my legs wrapped around him. He kissed me on my neck, then my shoulder, and moved to my breasts and nipples. I arched my back making my ass push against him.

"Mmmm . . . we should take this to the bedroom." With every step he took toward the bedroom he pumped his hard cock in me making me grunt louder and louder. His grip on me became more relaxed when he placed me on the bed. Sliding out of me then reaching for a bottle on the nightstand.

"What's that?" I asked curiously, lying on my back.

"Some lube. Flip over so I can make you feel even better."

I lay there not moving. My first thought was to kick his face in for insinuating that fucking me in my ass was going to make me feel good. I didn't want to disappoint him though. Nor did I want him to feel it was okay to do whatever to me. I sat up. "Umm, I've never done that before so . . ." I saw his eyes roll back a bit as if my inexperience was an epic fail. I didn't want him to push me to the side after this and treat me like some skank. I quickly flipped to my stomach and felt something warm running down the crack of my ass.

"Don't worry, baby, I'll be gentle I promise."

Then I felt the tip of his cock sliding across my asshole making sure the lube was all over. I remembered a porn actress said the more relaxed you are the better it would feel. He entered me with ease and I felt his body closer to my back.

Daniel moved slowly whispering at the back of my ear, "This is what I like . . . Ahh . . . you're so tight."

"Ahhh ahhh . . ." I rose up a little and started to rub on my clit. The lube he put on me brought a heat sensation to my touch. Pleasuring myself made me want him to stick his stiffness into me like he meant it. I pushed my butt back a little more.

"Oooh . . . yeah, push it back, baby . . . You like me fucking your tight ass . . . You gonna make me cum . . ."

He moved back a little and didn't move holding me tight; he was about to bust. We were in the doggie position and he gripped my ass cheeks moving me back and forth onto his manhood. After a few more strokes he pulled out and spilled his warm semen all over my ass. He got off the bed and snatched some tissues out of the box on the nightstand. After he wiped my ass cheeks clean, I turned over and he stood there wiping himself off next to the bed.

He looked over to me. "Would you like something to drink?"

My throat was parched. "Yes, please." I felt like a little schoolgirl having sex for the first time.

He left the room and returned with a glass of water. I sipped on it. Daniel got back into the bed and squeezed on my thigh.

"Are you ready for round two?" he asked with a grin.

I smiled then put the glass on the nightstand. "Do you have it in you?" I teased.

He pulled me close and got on top of me. "Let me show you." I felt his stiffness between my legs. He eased it into my flesh and I gasped.

"This is just as tight." He drove into me with conviction moaning with every stroke.

I would have slapped him for saying that, but with every inch he pushed into me made me weak. "Shut up and just fuck me . . . Stop talking . . . Ahhh ahhhh. Right there . . . right there . . . oh, Daniel . . ."

For the next few hours we rolled around like two honeymooners, sucking, fucking, licking, teasing, and best of all cumming. Daniel's kisses had passion every time he touched my lips or body. He paid attention to every part of my body not just the main attractions. After climaxing over and over again I finally had to give in and let him know I needed a break. He laughed at me then took me in his arms and held me until my eyes closed. Was he too good to be true? My eyes closed and I fell asleep feeling safe and wanted.

Sherry

17

Where the fuck is this bitch at? It was already eighty degrees in this hot-ass warehouse and it was only eight in the morning. The only thing on my mind was breakfast; my stomach was growling. I was waiting on some new chick Wayne contracted. I wished Cindy would actually stay around sometimes to see the bullshit I had to deal with, especially when Wayne got the girls. It seemed that all her input and ideas were discussed with Daniel instead of me.

All she did lately since she returned from Europe was bark orders into the phone. She hadn't called me up to talk or anything, just business. It was like our friendship didn't exist anymore; it was slowly diminishing. All she told me was that 'a deal' was on the table for some serious money. *What the fuck does that mean? I'm tired of being the only one doing most of the work while she runs around "making deals" as she says. She hasn't showed up on set or even sat down with me about new ideas to make us grow.*

For the past few months she'd been traveling to L.A., Miami, and Atlanta every other week just to meet Daniel. Why hadn't she asked me to tag along since I was the one on set and dealing with distributors? She must have thought I didn't see what she was doing: trying to fuck her way to the top. I understood she had to talk to Daniel, but fucking him was not even an option. When could I display my executive role and leave everything for someone else to handle? I was always stuck making sure her empire grew. She still hadn't answered me on the paperwork that was faxed to her about two other companies that my name wasn't attached to. What was that shit about?

My stomach growled again. I decided on heading to the deli to get a sandwich and some coffee while I waited for this chick. Twenty minutes passed and I returned with a sandwich to quiet my empty belly. I glanced at my phone and it was already past eight-thirty. *Where is this bitch?*

I pulled my phone out my back pocket and called Wayne. Three rings passed then it went straight to voice mail. "No, he did not just ignore me!" I said out loud, annoyed even more. "Fuck this shit. I'm not dealing with this crap." Just then the camera guy, Victor, walked in.

"Umm, you okay?" he asked.

"No work today, *papi*. No girl, no sex to shoot." I felt a little bad, but I shouldn't have been held accountable for something I had no control of.

"C'mon, Sherry, you can't call nobody else? I need this money. You know no work no pay." He was right.

"Nope, too late. Even if I call someone they ain't gonna get here 'til twelve. You know that would give us less than five hours of shooting. After three scenes the chick gonna say her body needs a break, then it will be 'my pussy's too sore.' You know the bullshit."

"Well, can you talk to Cindy about paying me for the day anyway since I showed up to work? It wasn't my fault that I can't shoot," Victor pleaded.

Every one of our staff was either a friend of a friend or a family member of a friend. I was fed up. I was constantly dealing with attitudes and dispositions. "I'm closing up shop," I said. I saw that he wasn't too happy about his unexpected day off.

"Okay." His voice was pathetic.

I walked over to Victor and patted him on the shoulder. "It'll be a'ight," I said hating for a grown-ass man to beg.

The door opened and a loud familiar voice echoed against the walls, "Yooooo . . ." Wayne walked in. He was looking around and scratching the top of his head. He walked over to me, throwing a fist bump to Victor walking out. "Umm, what's up? I thought you would be busy right about now. What happened, you ran ever'body out?" He laughed.

He was about to get a whole lot of mouth from me. "Maybe I would be fuckin' busy if you would've made sure to get yo' fuckin' ho of the week to show the fuck up!" My voice was loud.

He looked confused. "Hold up. First you gonna lower yo' voice; second, what the fuck you mean she ain't show up?"

"Did you not hear what I just said? Do you see me sitting in my fuckin' chair watching some bitch get her twat eaten out?" My blood was boiling. He thought he would do the same shit as Cindy do—bark orders. I smelled the reminiscence of a long night when I stepped closer to him waving my hand in his face.

"Let me call her and find out what's the deal. Give m—"

"Umm, ain't nobody here to shoot it. I sent Victor home. I'm done. I think you've forgotten who the hell is in charge in this bitch. You don't get to bark orders at me like Cindy. You act like you doing me a favor by bookin' one of yo' hoes. I'm not 'bout to keep yo' fuckin' hoes in line. That's yo' fuckin' job." I was fed up with all the crap I was expected to do while it seemed like everybody else wasn't worried about how the money was made, but sure as hell made sure they had it to spend.

"Wait, hold up. You more a part of this whole shit than me. I get what I want. I don't want to run shit like you crave so fuckin' much," he said walking over to the mirror. He checked himself out, touching the sides of his face.

"So 'cause I want to make sure shit is right with this company I'm overzealous?" I stepped back a bit and folded my arms across my chest. "You know what, Wayne, you right, fuck it. Yo' bitch ain't show up so you can explain that shit to Cindy and hear her fuckin' mouth. I'm outta here; my day is done. I should be more like y'all. Take trips and enjoy the pleasures outside this fuckin' company!" I stomped over to my director's chair and snatched my purse off of it.

"Trips? Cindy taking trips? Where? Is that why she wasn't callin' me back?"

"Oh, that's right, you wouldn't know 'cause if yo' ass ain't on set you nowhere to be found. Probably livin' yo' double life," I blurted out.

"Since when we close like that? When you had yo' chance you was scared. Listen just 'cause you overwork yo'self don't take that shit out on me. Where is Cindy anyway?"

"Ain't nobody want you in their bed!" I let out a nervous laugh. When I tasted his lips before they were sweet and I wanted more, but there was an unspoken rule between besties: "don't fuck or flirt with my man, ex-man, or any man I had a connection with at anytime while I'm living and breathing."

My thoughts must've been written on my face because he stepped closer to me. When I backed up my back was against the makeup station. His lips were now less than an inch away from mine. I wanted to taste his lips again. Cindy kept flashing in my mind causing my hesitation. Wayne didn't move any closer and said nothing. I knew what game he was playing. He wanted me to make the first move, that way his dirt wouldn't stain. All of his antics with Cindy and other bitches didn't matter anymore. It was about me now and after watching him all this time I needed to know how good he felt.

I felt his breath on my face, my heart was beating fast, and holding back was not an option I was considering. It was my turn to have what I wanted. I pushed my lips against his waiting for his reaction. As I suspected he quickly moved his hands to caress my ass and tongued me down like a hungry teenage boy. By the way he was pressing and groping on me, he must've wanted me even more.

I wasn't shy about what I wanted. I unbuckled his belt and dropped to my knees swallowing all of him. The tip of his cock was hitting the back of my throat. Although I was gagging I didn't stop. I sucked on him faster, moving my hand in a twisting motion up and down his shaft. I heard his moans but he wasn't there yet. I massaged his balls as I bobbed my head back and forth, making sure to look up at him. A few more strokes with my hand and he busted his nut directly in my mouth. I sucked every last drop out, and he backed away.

I returned to a standing position and wiped my lips with the back of my hand. He pulled his pants up and fastened his belt.

"Dammmmmnnn, girl, what you tryin'a to do to a brotha?" he asked a little winded. I didn't understand why he was out of breath; I was the one doing all the work.

"I gotta go. I'll see you." I looked into the mirror to check myself out making sure I didn't have any white dried up spots on my face. I grabbed a facial tissue from a box on the makeup station and wiped around my mouth looking into the mirror.

"I think you got every drop. I guess somebody been takin' notes instead of just watchin'." He laughed.

"Shut up." I giggled.

"Nah, seriously if I knew you had that type of skills I would have . . . hmmmm."

"Hmmm, nothin'. You wouldn't know how to handle this." I crumbled the tissue and threw it at him.

He laughed.

I looked over to the set. There was neatly made bed. I looked over to him and smiled.

"Ahh, so you want me now, huh?" He had this stupid grin on his face.

"Nope, just wanted a taste."

"A taste? Why not have it all when you can?" He watched me apply my lip gloss to my lips.

I heard a woman's voice, very high pitched and happy. Wayne quickly looked at his pants making sure his zipper was up. I didn't know who was approaching, but I took a quick glance at myself as I fixed my shirt.

"Okay, baby, I'll talk to you later." Cindy opened the door surprised to see both of us standing there. "Hey, I . . . I wasn't expecting to see you here, Wayne. Umm, where is everybody?"

I looked to Wayne. "You can answer her can't you?" I threw his ass straight to the lion.

He walked over to her and put his arm around her doing this childish motion of swaying side to side. "Ummm, you see what happened was—"

"Wayne, cut the shit. Sherry, can you please tell me what this nigga done fucked up!" Her tone wasn't so content anymore and she shrugged his arm off her shoulder.

"Wayne's chick didn't show up. I didn't—"

"So why you ain't on the phone tryin'a get somebody else? It ain't even noon yet."

Wayne stepped back a bit easing himself closer to the exit. I didn't want to get into an argument with her but I felt it coming. I was ready for her ass. This was the first time she'd shown up on set in a month.

"Wait, I know you ain't barking orders at me," I said sharply.

There was a brief pause before she answered, "Ain't *you* in charge of operations?"

I wanted to hit her, but I didn't. I took a deep breath and exhaled. She looked at me up and down.

"So what happened?" Cindy pressed.

"What happened?" I tilted my head back and screwed my face up. "Your fuckin' lame-ass nigga over here fucked up. He booked one of his hoes and they decided they wasn't working today. There is nobody else to call 'cause it's too late; by the time anyone gets here we're only gonna be able to shoot for 'bout three scenes. That ain't worth shit 'cause after edits we be lucky to get thirty minutes of somethin' good. I'm going the fuck home."

"Don't do that . . . it's not a good look for you. First, you supposed to want this money so it's kinda ridiculous to me that you wouldn't be on the phone tryin'a do somethin' 'bout it. And why would you book only one girl?" She was staring me down.

"Cindy, are you serious right now? When was the last time you been on set? When was the last time you even looked through some headshots? Oh yeah, that's right you was in Miami or was it L.A. with yo' new boo." I knew she wasn't going to like me putting her shit out there in front of Wayne.

Wayne was standing by the door listening and watching us. Cindy's eyes widened then she looked to Wayne. He started to walk toward us shaking his head.

"Who you fuckin'?" He stood directly in front of Cindy.

"Why are you up on me like that? Back up."

I stood there in silence. At that moment hitting her would have made my day.

"Why you so interested in who I'm fuckin'? You have no rights to me anymore so I can fuck whoever I please," she said with authority.

"Nah, I just wanna know."

I raised my eyebrows at him. He didn't just want to know; he wanted to make sure it wasn't someone he knew. "It ain't like he won't find out sooner or later," I threw in.

"It ain't none of your business, Wayne, neither yours, Sherry."

"You right. So why don't you handle some shit. I got somewhere to be." I grabbed my purse and passed by Wayne on the way out the door.

I stormed out of there with anger from the pit of my stomach. She had some nerve to walk in there and speak to me like her minion. This bitch didn't do shit anymore but jump every time Daniel summoned her. When I got to my car out front I hopped in, quickly throwing my Louis tote into the passenger seat of my BMW X6. I sat there for a minute contemplating what I would do to give her a lesson. That would be the last time she'd talk to me like that. I pulled my cell phone out my tote and sent a text to Wayne:

We should talk.

Crossing the line with him wasn't what I intended when I woke up this morning. Now I couldn't take it back and I sure as hell wasn't confessing to Cindy's dumb ass; guilt was not in my system and it wasn't in Wayne's either. I started the car and drove to BK thinking long and hard about Cindy. I used to be her best friend; now it all changed. I wasn't doing all this work while she played in the limelight. All the credit went to her while I busted my ass making sure "our company" was running smoothly.

Wayne

18

My phone started to buzz in my pocket. *Who the hell?* I didn't recognize the number when I looked at the screen. I was tempted not to answer and make them leave a message, but I was curious.

"Yo . . . "

It was a familiar voice. "What's up, Carla? What's goody?"

"Chillin', what's good with you?"

"Ain't shit, just tryin' to get this money. You know what I mean?"

"Yeah, yeah. I heard you fuckin' with some major ballers now. What's up, a bitch need an outlet." She laughed.

"I mean, if you sendin' some candy my way they gotta be on point. None of that 'round the way trick shit either."

"What you mean? All my bitches on point, nigga, what you talkin' 'bout?"

The last time I spoke to Carla she was supposed to get me some info on Daniel. But I never went to Chicago or even bothered to follow up because I was making money and had a new career to build. I wasn't worried about Daniel anymore; I was making my money.

I laughed. "I ain't heard from you in a minute. You still makin' it happen?"

"Hell yeah, you know nothin' don't stop me. But I heard you were into some porn shit now. Big star type shit."

"It ain't pop off yet the way it should, but I'm puttin' in some work."

"Yeah, nigga, you puttin' in some work a'ight . . ."

"Don't tell me you back on the good side, and lookin' for someone to control that ass!" I joked.

"Nigga, please, my dick bigger than yours."

We both busted out laughing.

"Nah, nigga, I wanted to ask you if you gettin' into that gay porn shit too 'cause—"

"Carla, I have mad respect for you, but I'm 'bout to hang the fuck up on yo' ass for talkin' out the side of yo' mouth. Why the fuck would you think I'm gettin' into that shit? Shit, the only porn I do is straight so what the fuck you talkin' 'bout?"

"Calm down, bro, I'm just fuckin' with you. But from what I hear shit don't make you look good no matter how many bitches you fuckin' on or off camera. I got to find out some things, you know how I do. After you called me way back when I ain't think nothin' of it. I thought it was some random white dude you just lucked up on."

"Let me guess, that ain't the case."

"Actually you lucked up on the right white nigga. He got some deep pockets and some major pull."

I was confused. *Major pull?* "What the fuck you talkin' 'bout, major pull? He runs some porn sites and threw my girl a bone to start her own shit. How you think I got on the screen? Now you comin' at me with some next shit. Just spit the shit out."

"You might want to watch who you fuck with in 'em videos." She giggled.

Now I was truly confused by her words. She was pissing me off now. "Yo, Carla, if you don't cut the shit I'ma definitely come see yo' ass in Chi. I don't understand what the fuck you tryin' to say to me. Is this nigga a fuckin' loaded mobster or some shit? Is he wanted and I shouldn't stand next to his ass or what?"

She was laughing harder now. I didn't like it. Was I the joke?

"Nigga, you probably can't even tell." She continued to laugh. "Nigga, you really need to make sure whoever you fuckin' on camera is a real fuckin' bitch."

"Carla, what the fuck you talkin' 'bout?"

"Hold on a minute."

Suddenly I received a media message. I opened it. It was a cover of one of the videos I did.

"Did you see what I just sent you?"

"Yeah, what the fuck? It's one of my video covers. What's the big deal? That ain't sayin' nothin'. Carla, stop wastin' my time."

"Nigga, look at the fuckin' words on the cover."

I opened up the message again. It said, "When Straight Men Can't Tell." I almost threw my phone against the fucking wall. What kind of shit was this? I never saw this. Cindy never showed me this.

"You playin' 'round, Carla. You know a nigga will shoot yo' ass over some shit like this."

"Bro, ain't nobody playin'. When one of my peoples brought this shit to me I slapped the shit outta 'em cause I thought the same. But when I looked it up on the Internet it was the same shit and other ones too."

"No, no, no, this motherfucker gonna—"

"Nigga, you may just want to bow out gracefully and take what you can now. I don't know how popular this shit is, but it sure is gettin' some heavy play 'round here. This dude Daniel ain't one to fuck with. He might look like an average, pretty white boy, but he knows people me and you can't reach. I'm tellin' you don't go off the handle. Shit, it's already out there and the niggas who know you ain't ever gonna see it unless they go that route. So get yo' money and bolt, my nigga."

"Do you hear yo'self, Carla? Are you tellin' me to hold back from bustin' a hole in that nigga head? He fuckin' played my ass. I gotta go."

"Yo, bro, don't do nothin' stupid. I'm tellin' you this man's reach is a whole lot longer and wider than ours. Trust me. One."

I didn't know what to do. I looked at my phone and Googled my name. It took a minute because my service sucked in Carmen's apartment. Slowly all my porn shit appeared. I clicked on the first link; it sent me to a transgender site that showed all my videos, Web cam shows, everything I ever did on camera. I kept clicking on links and they were all on gay or transgender sites. I couldn't believe it. What the hell was going on?

My stomach started to flip; flashes of me fuckin' those bitches ran through my mind. I started to gag. I thought I ate pussy, fucked pussy, fucked tits. I held my head, it started to pound. I dropped my phone to the floor.

The apartment door opened; I could hear Carmen's voice.

"Hey, baby, I hope you . . ." She saw me bent over holding my head. She quickly kneeled next to me. "Baby, what's wrong, you okay?"

I didn't say anything. I just shook my head from side to side.

"Baby, baby, what's wrong?" she asked with tears in her eyes. "Are you sick? Talk to me."

"Nah, baby, I ain't sick. I . . . I . . ." I pushed my phone toward her.

She picked it up and scrolled through the links I opened.

"I'm fucked, Carmen. I ain't fuckin' gay and definitely didn't know when I got into this shit that I would be fuckin' niggas who turned themselves into fuckin' females!" I sat up pressing my back against the sofa.

My eyes met hers and I thought it was strange when she didn't say anything. She just sat there like she wasn't even mad. I mean if I was her I would be pissed and ready to drag my ass to the clinic to make sure I wasn't carrying no disease like AIDS, HIV, STD, Syphilis, Hepatitis, anything. She sat there in silence. Was she in shock or did she know what was going on?

"Why aren't you sayin' nothin'? Are you fuckin' down with this bullshit? Did you know what Daniel was doin'?"

She looked away and stood up.

"Answer me; did you know anything 'bout this shit?"

"You should ask Cindy."

I was disturbed by her answer. Was she implying that Cindy did all this shit? I wouldn't believe that. Cindy wouldn't do that to me. She knew that would ruin me as a man, on the streets, to anyone who knew me. My rage was rising now. I stood up and walked closer to Carmen. She backed away like she knew more than what she was saying.

"Carmen, I swear to fuckin' God, you better tell me somethin' before I do somethin' I haven't done in a long-ass time. Trust me it won't be pretty."

"You should talk to Cindy."

I slapped her hard across the face. She instantly tried to run. I grabbed her by the hair and pulled her to the floor and punched her dead in the nose. Her gargled screams were loud. I punched her again, and again until I knocked her out. I paced the floor wondering what to do and who should I expose this to first. But all I was feeling was hurt and betrayal. *Did she really do this to me? With all we went through over the years, how could she do this to me? I thought we worked our shit out and was in a better place.*

I looked at Carmen laid out on the floor; her nose was bleeding. There was blood on her shirt. At first I was scared that I killed her by accident. Then I thought about when she woke up, she would definitely press charges. I grabbed my phone off the floor and stormed out the door. If she called the cops I wanted to be far away.

Sherry

19

It'd been a few days since I saw Wayne. I wanted to tell him everything, but my loyalty stayed with Cindy. There were so many nights she stayed up plotting and planning, making sure nothing would seem out of place. When she told me what she was doing, it seemed kind of ridiculous to go through hoops just to make him look like a fool. Although it was well deserved after all the crap he put her through I still thought she was going too far. It was one thing to make someone look like a fool, but fucking with somebody's integrity may get you killed.

There were times where I thought he would figure it all out, but Cindy knew her man. He only cared about pussy and money. I told Cindy that there would be a day when he wanted to see the covers of videos or have copies of it to give to his boys. Cindy was smart; she not only made sure that he had sex with real women, but also guided him to concentrate on his career and make as many videos as possible. It was cruel, but he deserved it.

I couldn't believe that I went that far with him now that I thought about it. I shouldn't have done what I did, but I wanted to hurt Cindy in a way. I would never confess to her what I did with him and I knew he wouldn't either so it was safe to say my secret was going to the grave with me.

I was sitting on the sofa when suddenly I heard banging at my door. I wasn't expecting anyone so I was a bit skeptical to open the door until I heard Wayne's voice.

"Sherry, open the door. It's me Wayne."

When I opened the door he bolted past me and called out Cindy's name. I looked at him like he was high.

"Wayne, what the fuck are you doin'? Cindy, don't live here. Why you actin' stupid?" I watched him move through my house like a madman. "Wayne, what the fuck are you doin'?"

"Sherry, I'ma ask you a question and you gotta tell me the truth. Okay?" He looked serious.

"Wayne, I don't have time for this shit. I gotta go somewhere," I lied and started to head into my room to grab my purse and sneakers.

He grabbed me by my wrist tight before I made two steps toward my room.

"Wayne, get the fuck off of me. I ain't Cindy. I will lock yo' stupid ass up. Let go of my hand." I stared into his eyes showing my seriousness.

"Nah, fuck that, you gonna tell me did you know what Cindy was doin'?"

I looked so confused. "What, fuckin' Daniel? She just started fuckin' him. Damn, Wayne, you flippin' out cause she not fuckin' you? Get over that shit. We all making some good money now, just sit back and collect. Besides, you like what you do now, don't you?" I had a little smirk on my face. I tried to turn my face so he wouldn't see it.

"Sherry, did you know about me fuckin' chicks who wasn't chicks? Did you know most of the videos I did were on gay porn sites? Transgender sites? My face on the fuckin' cover with the title 'When Straight Men Can't Tell,' did you know about that?"

I covered my mouth to hide my smirk, but my eyes told him all he needed to know.

"I should beat the shit outta you right now."

I backed up and slowly walked toward my bedroom keeping my eyes on him. He didn't move toward me, he just looked at me. Then suddenly he lunged. I ducked and dove into the bedroom and slammed the door in his face.

"Bitch, open this fuckin' door. I swear—"

"Fuck you. I'm callin' the fuckin' cops!" I screamed.

"With what phone, bitch? Yo' phone out here. Stupid bitch! I don't have to be nowhere. I'ma wait for yo' ass to come out so I can beat the shit out of you. Damn, I thought we was cool. You sucked my fuckin' dick like we cool. Or did you just want a taste of 'em fabricated pussies?"

I heard every word, but I wasn't going to respond. My answers would only fuel the fire. I just hoped he would eventually leave. A few minutes went by and he continued to shout at the door. I remained silent. Then abruptly a crashing sound was heard. I put my ear to the door and I heard another crash. *I know this motherfucker not breakin' up my shit,* I thought.

"Wayne, you better not be doin' what I think you doin' cause—" Immediately I felt the door shake and a big bang, forcing me to back away. Then another big bang, this time the door flew open. I searched the room with my eyes for something to throw at him, but it was too late. The last thing I saw was his fist then everything went black.

Cindy

20

It was almost two on a Sunday afternoon and I hadn't heard from Sherry yet. She was supposed to call me with information about our shoot for tomorrow. I wanted to be on set because we were testing out some new sex toys that I developed. I had my hand in almost every part of the sex industry. With Daniel at my side I was unstoppable. He guided me with everything. He was everything I wanted in a man: the looks, style, charisma, and most of all the business mind of a mogul. I didn't care about his skin color. Sherry sure did remind me of it.

I picked up my phone, scrolled to her pic in my favorite list, and touched her number. After two rings I expected her to pick up, but it kept ringing and went straight to voice mail. I left a message for her to call me. It was strange that she didn't pick up. After our little tiff I realized I was taking advantage of her so I told her to hire an assistant; that way she could get the time off that she wanted and she didn't have to be overwhelmed with the everyday stuff. She could concentrate on the importance of growing the company.

An hour passed and still she hadn't called me back. I tried to call her again. If she didn't pick up I was going over there.

Suddenly a voice said, "Cindy, he . . . he knows."

At first I didn't know what she was talking about. *He knows? Who the fuck is she talking about?* Her voice was shaky. I could feel something was wrong.

"Sherry, did you just wake up or something? You don't sound like yourself."

She was crying. She couldn't get a word out.

"Sherry, are you home?"

Between the crying and sniffling she got out the word, "Yes."

I threw my sneakers on and grabbed my purse then hurried to Sherry's. On the way there I couldn't for the life of me figure out what was going on with her. It only took about twenty minutes to get to her place.

I stepped out the cab and noticed two empty cop cars sitting in front of her building. Because she lived in the hood still I didn't think it was anything. I told her ass she needed to move. It wasn't like she didn't have the money, now. I got off the elevator and noticed the police were standing in front of Sherry's open apartment door. I slowly walked toward the apartment.

"Excuse me, miss, do you know Sherry Pace?" a short, baldheaded man asked. He was dressed in a suit so it was obvious that he was a detective.

I didn't know what to say at first. I stood there in shock. "Where is Sherry?" I said loudly.

"Miss, everything is okay but we have a few questions for you before you can step into the apartment. Can you come with me, please?"

Now I was really confused. "I'm not going anywhere until I see Sherry." I folded my arms across my chest.

"Miss, you'll get to see your friend, but we need to ask you a few questions. That's all."

I didn't care what questions he had for me because I had nothing to do with whatever happened here. I was there not even two minutes and it was like I was being interrogated for something I had no clue of. I was getting upset at this point so I yelled for Sherry. "Sherry, please tell these motherfuckers I'm not the fuckin' suspect here!" Unexpectedly I pushed through him and dashed into the apartment.

Sherry was sitting on the sofa surrounded by two more guys in suits. She and the detectives around looked to me causing all the commotion.

"Miss, you can't—"

The detective tried to hold me back, but Sherry finally spoke, "No, please let her in."

The guys in suits stopped holding me back and let me closer to her. When I saw her it was horrific. Her eyes were swollen, blood was oozing out of her nose, and you could see the bruising on her face starting to appear. It looked like she went six rounds in an MMA fight with Ronda Rousey. Her face was fucked up. The place was a wreck. Everything was smashed; the big-screen TV was now on the floor, the coffee table was flipped over, and broken glass littered the floor; it was terrible. Before I could say anything the paramedics arrived and shooed me out the way and into the sights of the detectives.

"Miss, can you give me your name and step out of the apartment? This is now a crime scene and you may hurt yourself. Come on, follow me." He took my hand and led me out the door.

"Cindy Walker."

"Do you know who would try to hurt your friend?"

"No." I kept my answers short and to the point.

"There's no one who comes to mind you think may want to do this? Maybe an ex or someone she worked with?" Detectives always thought they were smart, asking me the same damn question in different way. How stupid did he think I was?

"No." I saw the paramedics putting Sherry on a gurney and strapping her in. "What hospital are they takin' her to?"

"Kings County probably."

"What happened? Did someone break in?"

"From the looks of it, it could be a home invasion but your friend said they wore masks."

"Listen, I want to get to the hospital to be with my friend. Please let me go." My leg was shaking; I wanted to leave in a hurry.

"Sure, but we may need to speak to you again. Someone will be at the hospital shortly to get all your information. Thank you." He turned his back and walked back into the apartment examining the entrance from the inside.

I rushed down the steps instead of taking the elevator to catch the ambulance. When I got downstairs the paramedics were closing the back doors and a crowd began to build outside the building.

"Excuse me, excuse me, can I ride in the back with her?"

"Are you family?" the fat dude asked.

"Yes, I'm her sister," I said quickly.

"Okay, get in the back." He waddled over to the back and opened the door.

I hopped in and sat beside Sherry. Both paramedics were up front. I took her hand and squeezed it. Her eyes were beginning to close shut. "I'm here, Sherry. I'm here."

"He knows, Cindy. He found out." Her words were muffled from the swelling of her lips. She continued slowly, "I don't know how, but he did . . . I didn't say nothin'." She started to cry.

I held her hand and delicately moved my finger against her skin. I was thinking hard as to why she said what she said. I stayed quiet and listened to her groan as the ambulance caught every pothole down Flatbush Avenue.

Then it hit me like a ton of bricks—Wayne. *Holy shit! This is my entire fault. If I wasn't so fucking busy on Daniel and this fucking money I would have figured a way to get him away from here. Oh, my God, I feel so bad! He'll be gunning for me next.*

The back doors of the ambulance flew open. I didn't even notice when we stopped.

"Okay, sweetie, let's get you looked at."

I jumped out of the ambulance and watched them take her out. As they rolled her into the hospital, my mind was only concentrating on thing: *How can I stop Wayne?* To be honest I was scared out my pants and didn't want my face to be anyone's punching bag. The paramedics stepped away from us for a moment to check her in. I leaned into her and whispered in her ear, "Don't say nothing else to the cops. I'll get it handled. He won't have a chance to do this again." I kissed her red, puffy, swollen forehead and told her I would be back. She tried to grab on to me so I wouldn't leave, but her strength wasn't capable of doing it.

"Hey, where you going?" I heard the paramedic yelled out to me.

"I'll be back." I almost ran out of there because I didn't want to bump into any cops on this case.

I flagged down a livery cab and got in. I wanted to go back home to pack a suitcase, but instead I headed into the city, stopping at the Marriott Marquis in Midtown Manhattan. I knew it was crazy to be that far from Sherry right now, but I also knew she would be safer if I stayed away. I checked into the hotel first to clear my head and figure out how I could fix this mess.

Carmen

21

Damn, my face hurts. My eyes were opening slightly finally. I didn't know how long I was out. I got up slowly; my head was spinning in every direction. I put my back against the wall to support me in case I stumbled from my dizziness.

Oh my God, how the fuck I'm going to explain this shit to Daniel? I hobbled to the front door slowly and locked it. My head was pounding. I looked into the mirror; I had a small cut over my right eye; the right side of my face was starting to swell. I looked to the kitchen; it seemed real far from where I was standing and the hurt I was feeling. I used the wall as a crutch and slowly made it to the kitchen. I pulled out some ice from the freezer and wrapped it up in a dish towel and put it on my face.

I sat there thinking how I did not see this coming. When Cindy told me what she was doing I tried to talk her out of it, but all the hurt she endured with him she wanted payback in the worst way. She figured the best way was to damage his manhood and fuck his mind up all at the same time. I couldn't stop her nor did I feel I should. I guessed I got caught up too. I figured I would be able to tell Wayne about the true me and he wouldn't take any offense to it because he was fucking females like me all along.

There was a knock at my door. I was too scared to move. It chimed again.

Then a soft voice was heard: "It's me Cindy. Open the door."

I moved slowly toward the door and opened it. Her eyes said it all. She was surprised to see me in the condition I was. Before she entered the apartment she asked, "What happened to you?" She stepped in looking around and moving real slow. "Carmen, what happened to you?"

"You better sit down." She helped me to the sofa. "It was Wayne. He did this. He found out and showed his anger."

"Wait, hold on. Wayne did this to you too?"

"What you mean me too?" I removed the ice pack on my face stared at her.

"He saw Sherry too. It looks like she got the worst of it. She's at Kings County now." She stood up. "How did he know you knew? Why was he even here?"

"I didn't tell him anything. I don't know how he knew. But there's something else I have to tell you." It took a lot to tell her who I truly was.

"Something else?" She turned to me and stood directly in front of me.

"Yeah . . ." I was hesitant to say anything because I didn't want to get hit again. I scooted to the other side of the sofa. "I was seeing Wayne secretly."

"You were fuckin' Wayne? How long? When did it start?"

The questions were spitting out at a mile an hour. I didn't think she cared after she engineered the whole scheme. She was the one that wanted to hurt him. I guessed she didn't expect anyone else to get hurt.

"Yes, I was, but I thought you wanted to hurt him."

"So that made it okay for you to start fuckin' him?"

"Why would you even care since you started fuckin' Daniel?" Her face turned red. Did she not think he would tell me? Daniel loved me and would never keep me in the dark.

"Fuckin' Daniel? What does that even matter? Did you send Wayne to Sherry's?"

"I think he was there looking for you." I put the ice back on my face.

"Carmen, where is Daniel? I think we need to call him don't you?" She cocked her head to the side. "Where is he?"

"I don't know. You know him; he may not even be in town. My head's killing me."

"I bet it is," she said in a low voice taking a seat on the opposite side of me. "Tell me the truth, Carmen, who is Daniel to you?"

"I don't think you want to know."

"I do."

"He was my everything. I've known him since I was sixteen. He's taken care of me for years."

"Is he your pimp?"

"You lucky I'm hurt or else I would've slapped the shit out of you for saying that." I wanted to throw the ice at her, but I was in too much pain.

"Why didn't you say that to me? Why didn't Daniel tell me?"

"There was no reason to. We were all making money including you."

"So why did you help me? What was the bigger picture?"

"I think Daniel should explain that to you. My phone is over there." I pointed toward the kitchen.

She walked over to the kitchen and picked up her phone.

"Who is this?"

I didn't think she would even recognize the picture as my wallpaper.

"Who is this Daniel's hugging and why is it on your phone?"

It was time to fess up to everything. In a low voice I answered, "It's me and him when we first met." I waited.

She said nothing; she was still staring at the picture.

"It was before I changed."

"Before you changed? You're a fuckin' man? You're a fuckin' man?" She couldn't believe it. Cindy kept repeating the same question over and over again. I turned my head and closed my eyes for a moment. I felt dizzy.

Suddenly I felt a sharp sting to the back of my head. I moved forward as fast I could and dropped to the floor. I tried to turn around, but Cindy was already on top of me moving a sharp knife in and out of me. I couldn't breathe. I struggled to get her off of me, but I was weak. The knife moved swiftly in and out of my back. She held my head to the floor as she stabbed me. I was getter weaker. I couldn't fight anymore. I was fading. My soul was moving outward and I was inhaling eternal acceptance and happiness.

Cindy

22

Carmen wasn't moving. Her body was limp. Blood was all over her back and the floor. I didn't know what came over me. My mind and body went black when I heard her say it was her in the picture with Daniel. It was a picture of a young boy with long hair in a female stance with a younger Daniel holding on to his waist in a loving way.

The thought of Daniel being with her as a man made me feel dirty, used, and most of all hurt because he lied to me. How could he lie to me? I thought we were building a future together. I wanted a future with him. I loved him. Was it all a lie? Why did he help me? I had to talk to him. I had to call him.

My hands were shaking. I dropped the knife and stood up. I rushed into the kitchen and opened the faucet over the sink. The warm water washed away the blood on my hands. I vigorously pumped the hand soap into my palm and washed my hands again. I dried my wet hands on the sides of my pants. I rushed over to my purse in the living room and pulled out my phone. Quickly, I called Daniel. My hands were still shaking. My lips were trembling. I searched my bag for the box of cigarettes and pulled one out.

As I lit the cigarette, Daniel answered, "Hey, baby, what's up? I was just thinking about you."

"Are you in town?"

"Yeah, for a few hours. Why?"

"You need to come to Carmen's now. There's something wrong."

"Is Carmen okay?"

"Yeah, she's happy. How soon can you be here?"

"In twenty minutes." The phone went dead.

I went through half the pack of smokes waiting for him. I kept looking at the body waiting for Carmen to move, but I knew she wouldn't.

There was a knock at the door. I jumped. I walked over to the door and looked through the peephole. It was him. I knew once I opened this door there would be a price to pay. I opened the door.

"Hey," he greeted me with a hug and a kiss on the cheek. Then abruptly he pushed me away and ran over to Carmen. "Carmen . . . Carmen . . . Call the ambulance." He was screaming.

I slammed the front door.

"Daniel, she's gone . . . or maybe I should say he's gone. When were you going to tell me you were bisexual?" I walked into the kitchen as he held his precious Carmen in his arms with tears leaving his eyes.

"Oh, my God, Cindy, what did you do? How did you get to this point?"

"No, before you start asking questions you're gonna answer mine first." I started to pull out the drawers of the cabinet searching for a bigger knife. "Why did you help me, Daniel? Did you know your fuckin' he-she bitch was fuckin' Wayne?"

"Call a fucking ambulance, Cindy! Damn, what the fuck!" His tears were full blown now, streaming down his face.

"She's fuckin' dead, Daniel, get fuckin' past it! Answer me or you're gonna be answering to the cops!" I sliced my shoulder; then I sliced my stomach and grabbed my phone out my back pocket and prompted the 911 emergency number on the screen. "You better answer because if you don't I'll call the cops and you will go down for all of this including my death."

"Cindy, please there's no reason to hurt yourself. I love you. My sexuality wasn't a factor anymore. You changed all that. That's why I didn't care when she started fuckin' Wayne. Please believe me. I was going to tell you the next time I saw you. Please . . . Please." He left Carmen and headed toward the kitchen.

I held the knife out in front of me. "You lied. You fuckin' lied. Tell me, Daniel, why did you help me? Why, Daniel, why?" I waved the knife.

"Okay, Cindy, okay, just put the knife down. I'll tell you . . ." He stepped closer, but I motioned forward letting him know I wasn't bluffing.

"Cindy, it's way bigger than just this. I needed you because you were clean. New name with nothing attached, no red flags, nobody watching, easier for you to send money out the country than my friends."

"Friends? Daniel, what the fuck are you talkin' about? I don't know your friends! Daniel, stop lying!' I started to wave the knife at him.

He jumped back and reached into his pants pocket.

"Slow, motherfucker, slowly. What you got in yo' pocket?"

"Cindy, I want to show you. It's my phone. Calm down, it's just my phone."

"Give it to me. Do you think I'm stupid? Who you gonna call?"

"Cindy scroll through the contacts, you'll see the name Swiss. Dial it."

I did what he said. It was an automated system of a bank in Switzerland. He told me to enter an account number. I did. The robotic voice said, "$2,657,000 is your current balance."

"What does this mean?"

"It's all yours if you want and there's more. We just need to get out of here now." All his tears were dried up now.

"Why are you telling me this?"

"Because, I love you."

I didn't know if it was his words or the blood I was losing from my stomach making me dizzy. My hand let go of the knife and before I could fall Daniel caught me in his arms.

"Let's go, Cindy, let's go. We need to leave now. We can't be here when the cops show up."

I heard his words and I felt his strength holding me, but I was still trying to resist. Then the front door opened. I saw Wayne rushing in. I leaned on the counter to hold myself up. Daniel instantly moved to protect me and grabbed the knife tucking it out of eyesight.

"You fuckin' bitch! You set this shit all up! You knew I was fuckin' men! What were you trying to do to . . ." He spotted Carmen on the floor and rushed over to her.

"She's dead."

"What the fuck!" Wayne put his hands up in the air.

His face was priceless when he saw me standing there with Daniel. He didn't want to believe it.

"Are you gonna miss her? Oh well, you wouldn't of liked her after you found out anyway!" I chuckled, which quickly led to a groan of pain. He was more confused.

He looked at me with a distasteful smirk. "You think shit funny, huh? Did you want to ruin me? Did you not think this through? You know if I found out I would kill yo' ass. Is that why you hidin'? I'ma fuckin' kill you, bitch. Ain't nobody gonna recognize yo' ass when I get through, trust me. That's why I shoulda kept beatin' yo' ass that way you woulda been too fuckin' scared to pull some shit like this."

Wayne's threats gave me power. "It doesn't feel good does it? Someone betraying you, taking you for granted, using you . . . oh, yeah . . ." I slid Carmen's phone off the counter. "Pick it up; look at the wallpaper on there."

At first he didn't move, but then he walked over closer to the countertop and picked up the phone. He touched the screen on the phone. His head cocked to the side.

"What the fuck is this?"

"It's yo' fuckin' girl, Carmen, before the change, you dumb ass! Now how you feel. Not only did I fuck yo' head up, but it seems that yo' girl had the same motive."

He looked at the picture then at us. He dropped the phone and lunged for me. Daniel pushed me out of the way and held the knife up. There was a loud moan.

I eased up from the floor and saw Wayne on the counter-top and blood on Daniel's hand. Wayne slid off the counter with the knife in his chest.

"Daniel, what did you do?" My body went limp and I fell to the floor. I couldn't keep my eyes open. I allowed myself to be vulnerable at the worst time.

My eyelids were heavy and the bright lights forced them to stay low. *Was it a dream? Why can't I move my hand?* I tried to move my legs; it felt like something was holding them. I struggled to open my eyes; then I heard a familiar voice.

"Is everything okay?"

That sounds like Daniel. I tried to move my hands.

"Yeah, no big deal, only a few stitches here and there."

Screams exited my mouth.

"She's waking up. Do you want me to keep her down for a while? I can give her a little more," a tall white man in green scrubs said.

Forcing my eyes to open wider, I could see Daniel next to the man in scrubs. *Shit, what the fuck is this? Where am I?* I lifted my head and saw that my ankles and hands were strapped. It looked like I was in a hospital room ready for surgery. I started to scream again. "Daniel, Daniel, please I won't say nothin' please." I started crying hysterically. Fighting to move my hands and feet I continued to plead. "Please, Daniel, please."

"Can you leave us for a minute?" Daniel looked to the man in scrubs.

"Yeah, sure, no problem. I'll make sure nobody comes in here. Take all the time you need."

Through my tears I screamed for the man to help me. He never turned around. He shook Daniel's hand and walked out the room closing the door behind him.

"Cindy, you got to calm down. Nobody's here to hurt you. You have—"

"Untie me!" I screamed at him.

"Cindy, you can't leave here and go back home. Do you remember what you did?"

"Are you crazy? What I did?" With all my effort I tried to strike him. I was limited to how much I could lift my hands. I realized it was fruitless to try. I stopped trying.

"Cindy, do you not remember?" he asked me again.

I lay there in silence. Tears flowed out my eyes. *What the fuck is he gonna do to me? Is he gonna kill me? What did he do with me already?* Crazy questions entered my mind. I closed my eyes wishing that it was just a nightmare and I would wake up soon.

I felt soft tissue moving across my face. Daniel was wiping away my tears.

"Cindy, it's okay. Everything is okay. It will be fine."

"Noooo, noooo." Flashes of Sherry's bruises, the blood on my hands, the knife in my hand, Wayne's body falling to the floor. I started to shake my head. I heard the buckles of my straps coming undone. First my hands, then my feet; immediately I wiped my eyes and tried to sit up.

"Whoa, you shouldn't do that." He lightly pushed back on my shoulders.

"No, I want to go."

"Cindy, where you going? You can't go back home. You'll be arrested for the murder of Carmen and Wayne. Do you want to live the rest of your in prison?"

"I . . . I . . . I didn't kill . . ." I covered my face with my hands and screamed.

"Cindy, you stabbed Carmen. I—"

"Daniel, I don't want to go to prison for the rest of my life. Please, please." I begged. I couldn't believe what I did.

"Okay, but you must never come back to New York. Never."

"What about my business? I worked so hard; how can I just throw it away?"

He shook his head. "Hmmm, you worried about your business? You can forget about your business for now; leave it in the hands of Sherry. She can handle it."

I looked at my arm; it had bandages wrapped around it and my stomach did too. I didn't know what to do. I was in pain.

"Cindy, I'm sending you to Europe. You can't be seen in New York. The cops will question you."

"I don't even know what really happened. Maybe I should just talk to the cops."

"Really? Okay, well, I'll see you then. I'm leaving and if you don't come with me now, I won't be able to help you at all."

"Why can't you get me a high-profile lawyer who will surely get me out? I don't want to leave everything and everyone I know." I didn't know if I should trust him. I couldn't remember all that happened; it was a blur in my mind. At the moment I only saw flashes of that night.

I had to trust him. I couldn't see myself behind bars. I looked down at myself; I had a hospital gown on. I moved to get off the gurney.

"Cindy, wait . . ." He helped me off the gurney.

"Let's go, Daniel. If we have to go, let's go."

Daniel helped me to the door and held me close. After we left the building we got into a car. I had no clue where we going. All I knew was that Daniel was going to get me far away from here. I didn't want to remember anything.

I didn't speak during the ride. We arrived at a small private hanger in Long Island. Daniel got out the car and walked up to a man standing by the small jet. I didn't have anything on but the hospital gown. I didn't want to get out of the car. I was feeling uncomfortable. I saw Daniel walking back to the car. The door opened.

"Cindy, c'mon."

I grabbed his hand and he walked me to the jet. I hoped Daniel's plan to keep me safe and out of prison was genuine. I was connected to him for life now. I walked up the steps and boarded the plane with only one question on my mind: *What will my life turn into now?*

ORDER FORM
URBAN BOOKS, LLC
97 N18th Street
Wyandanch, NY 11798

Name (please print):_____

Address: _____

City/State: _____

Zip: _____

QTY	TITLES	PRICE

Shipping and handling: add $3.50 for 1st book, then $1.75 for each additional book.

Please send a check payable to:

Urban Books, LLC

Please allow 4-6 weeks for delivery

ORDER FORM
URBAN BOOKS, LLC
97 N18th Street
Wyandanch, NY 11798

Name (please print):_____

Address: _____

City/State: _____

Zip: _____

QTY	TITLES	PRICE
	16 On The Block	$14.95
	A Girl From Flint	$14.95
	A Pimp's Life	$14.95
	Baltimore Chronicles	$14.95
	Baltimore Chronicles 2	$14.95
	Betrayal	$14.95
	Bi-Curious	$14.95
	Bi-Curious 2: Life After Sadie	$14.95
	Bi-Curious 3: Trapped	$14.95
	Both Sides Of The Fence	$14.95
	Both Sides Of The Fence 2	$14.95
	California Connection	$14.95

Shipping and handling: add $3.50 for 1st book, then $1.75 for each additional book.
Please send a check payable to:
Urban Books, LLC
Please allow 4-6 weeks for delivery

ORDER FORM
URBAN BOOKS, LLC
97 N18th Street
Wyandanch, NY 11798

Name (please print):_____

Address: _____

City/State: _____

Zip: _____

QTY	TITLES	PRICE
	California Connection 2	$14.95
	Cheesecake And Teardrops	$14.95
	Congratulations	$14.95
	Crazy In Love	$14.95
	Cyber Case	$14.95
	Denim Diaries	$14.95
	Diary Of A Mad First Lady	$14.95
	Diary Of A Stalker	$14.95
	Diary Of A Street Diva	$14.95
	Diary Of A Young Girl	$14.95
	Dirty Money	$14.95
	Dirty To The Grave	$14.95

Shipping and handling: add $3.50 for 1st book, then $1.75 for each additional book.

Please send a check payable to:
Urban Books, LLC
Please allow 4-6 weeks for delivery

ORDER FORM
URBAN BOOKS, LLC
97 N18th Street
Wyandanch, NY 11798

Name (please print): _____

Address: _____

City/State: _____

Zip: _____

QTY	TITLES	PRICE
	Gunz And Roses	$14.95
	Happily Ever Now	$14.95
	Hell Has No Fury	$14.95
	Hush	$14.95
	If It Isn't love	$14.95
	Kiss Kiss Bang Bang	$14.95
	Last Breath	$14.95
	Little Black Girl Lost	$14.95
	Little Black Girl Lost 2	$14.95
	Little Black Girl Lost 3	$14.95
	Little Black Girl Lost 4	$14.95
	Little Black Girl Lost 5	$14.95

Shipping and handling: add $3.50 for 1st book, then $1.75 for each additional book.
Please send a check payable to:
    Urban Books, LLC
Please allow 4-6 weeks for delivery

ORDER FORM
URBAN BOOKS, LLC
97 N 18th Street
Wyandanch, NY 11798

Name (please print):_____

Address: _____

City/State: _____

Zip: _____

QTY	TITLES	PRICE
	Loving Dasia	$14.95
	Material Girl	$14.95
	Moth To A Flame	$14.95
	Mr. High Maintenance	$14.95
	My Little Secret	$14.95
	Naughty	$14.95
	Naughty 2	$14.95
	Naughty 3	$14.95
	Queen Bee	$14.95
	Say It Ain't So	$14.95
	Snapped	$14.95
	Snow White	$14.95

Shipping and handling: add $3.50 for 1st book, then $1.75 for each additional book.

Please send a check payable to:

Urban Books, LLC

Please allow 4-6 weeks for delivery

ORDER FORM
URBAN BOOKS, LLC
97 N. 18th Street
Wyandanch, NY 11798

Name (please print): _____

Address: _____

City/State: _____

Zip: _____

QTY	TITLES	PRICE
	Spoil Rotten	$14.95
	Supreme Clientele	$14.95
	The Cartel	$14.95
	The Cartel 2	$14.95
	The Cartel 3	$14.95
	The Dopefiend	$14.95
	The Dopeman Wife	$14.95
	The Prada Plan	$14.95
	The Prada Plan 2	$14.95
	Where There Is Smoke	$14.95
	Where There Is Smoke 2	$14.95

Shipping and handling: add $3.50 for 1st book, then $1.75 for each additional book.

Please send a check payable to:

Urban Books, LLC

Please allow 4-6 weeks for delivery